CURSED BLOODLINES

MJ Donohue

CONTENTS

PRE-WORD

Do you believe in destiny? The dictionary defines it as "something that is to happen or has happened to a particular person or thing; lot or fortune." Some call it fate; others call it karma. The author Stephen King calls it Ka.

"Ka is a mysterious force that leads all living and unliving creatures—the approximate equivalent of destiny or fate. Ka can be considered to be a guide, a destination, but is certainly not a plan, at least not one that is known by mortals. Ka is not necessarily a force of good or evil; it manipulates both sides, and seems to have no definite morality of its own." Stephen King's Ka is by far the one that inspired this part of the story.

PART ONE

THE BEGINNING

1

A long time ago, 3500 miles off the coast of California, there was an island, now known as the Hawaiian Islands. Stretching about 6,423 square miles, this island was named Atheria. As far as anyone can remember, the Kastle clan ruled the island. The kings and queens were always fair, hardworking people, and always did what was best for their subjects. Atheria had its fair share of plights and disasters, just like any other civilization. They had their invaders during the 3rd century, and the rat plague not long after that. But they always pulled through and came out a stronger people because of it.

In the early 5th century, during the reign of King Alexander Kastle and Queen Scarlett, a great plague swept their kingdom, and Alexander grew very concerned. Hundreds of villagers were getting sick and dying, so the king called the entire kingdom to a mandatory hearing at the castle gate. In his speech, the king told the people to batten down and prepare for the worst. He announced that he was closing the castle and wanted all of them to prepare enough rations for at least a year and to keep to just their close family until this plague ended. He also said that every full moon, he would send his healers out to assess the situation. The people were not happy, but they knew the king was doing what he thought was right. Alexander ordered the guards to close and secure the gate and for all of his staff to confine themselves to their own floors and prepare for the long haul with the limited rations he supplied. Seoul, the wizard, put an enchantment on the castle, closing it off to the outside world. Months went by, and the healers kept reporting that things seemed to be getting worse. After about a year, the situation appeared to be at its worst; thousands were dead, and even more were sick.

The rations fell short, and the king had to ask his family to give some of their rations to help feed the staff low on their own rations. Alexander's son Mathias, who was only twelve when all this began, told his father he was not giving any of his food up to "peasants" and people he deemed "lower" than him. He started sneaking into the kitchen at night and hoarding food in his room after his father's request.

Mathias was a spoiled boy who thought he was entitled to everything and had to earn nothing. He was a tall boy for his age and scrawny, with dark blonde hair and built like his mother. His bright blue eyes always won the trust of everyone when he was caught doing something wrong and would lie to avoid consequences. That would change with age. He always trained hard, but only because his father pushed him to do so. He preferred to train with his double axes and liked to think he was better than all the knights' children training with him, without realizing they went soft on him so that he could win. They knew of his temper and knew as a sore loser, he would find a way to get back at them.

The kingdom was nearing the two-year mark of the plague, food and supplies were nearly exhausted, and the king was stressed about how long they could survive. One morning, Alexander's healers returned from their weekly scouting of the kingdom with somewhat good news. No new cases of the plague, many more had died, and many more were still sick, but no new cases, and many of the children seem to be developing an immunity to the disease. The king was happy with this news, but not willing to cut the reins just yet. He was afraid that this might just be a momentary pause before it comes swirling back to life with a vengeance, claiming more lives than it already had. The problem was that all their supplies were so low that it might start a rebellion. He decided in 12 days he'd have the healers go out, and if things were still the same, he would lift the ban. Twelve days later, the healers went out, and two days later they returned with the same news: no new cases to report. Alexander and Scarlett gathered all the healers, aides, and a select group of guards. The guard's job was twofold: protect the king, queen, and the healers, along with putting people who were too sick out of their misery, a harsh choice but one that was best for the kingdom.

Alexander and his family set out of the castle after Seoul rescinded the enchantment and headed for the villages. As they were leaving, Scarlett told the king she needed to check on her sister and her family to see how badly they were affected. As they headed deeper into the village, things got bleaker from home to home the further they got away from the castle. Near the edge of the village stood a small, quaint home that Scarlett pointed out as her sister's.

Scarlett was tall and thin with long, dark blonde hair down to her waist, with wisps of gold mixed with the twinkling midday sun. She had soft, sugar-sweet lilac lips and a sculptured figure, strong yet soft in its own way. Her delicate ears framed a short-pointed nose.

She dismounted her horse and went towards the curtain that was hung as a door. She pushed it aside and called her sister's name, "Kar……" but before she finished, a young child lunged at her, swinging a sword at her head, bound to take it off. With a quickness only a few had seen, the king was off his horse and at his wife's side. His sword moved with such ferocity and speed that it was barely seen by anyone in the party. With two swift moves, Alexander had disarmed the young boy and had him pinned under his foot.

As the king was bringing down his sword, Scarlett screamed, "Alexander, STOP!!!"

"He was about to take your head off, Scarlett. Why should I stop?" Scarlett looked at the boy and asked, "Boy, what is your name?"

"My name is Roland, and this is my home. Go away. Leave us alone. I won't let you steal any more food from us! Let me go!" he screamed, straining to breathe as the king's heavy foot was restricting his ability to pull any air into his lungs.

The king was a very large man, 6' 9" tall and almost just as wide, with a long black beard that matched his shoulder-length black hair. Both his beard and hair had dark red strands of such a deep shade, they resembled the fine wine he was served at dinner. His arms were as thick as the old ironwood growing in his forests, and his shoulders so broad that people actually believed he could hold the whole world upon them.

The queen looked at the boy and spoke slowly and softly, hoping to calm him down. "Roland, your mother is my sister. Do you not recognize who we are?? Where are your mother and father?" Scarlett glanced at her husband to let the boy up. He slowly lifted his titanic foot from the boy's chest while keeping his hand on the hilt of his sword, not trusting the boy's intentions.

The boy took a giant breath to refill his lungs, and took a few moments to gather his thoughts, then finally spoke, "My father has died from the plague, my sister also, but my mother is still holding on, no thanks to our king and queen abandoning us out here to die. I figured you were the thieves who heard about my father's death and were here to rob us of the little we have left to eat." Tears rolled down his dirty face, streaking through the dirt and muck covering his entire body. "Mother isn't going to make it, but I've been doing everything I can to try to k–k-k-keep her alive…" he sobbed uncontrollably. He dropped to his knees; they could tell from the haggard look on his face that he was exhausted.

The king stood up and said to the boy, "We did not abandon you, child, we told everyone that this plague would take time to pass and only god would decide who lives, and who dies."

The boy dropped to his knees, mostly because of exhaustion but also in respect to the king, and said, "I'm sorry, my king, I didn't know it was you. Does this mean the plague is over and you can cure my mother?"

"There is no cure, boy, we will have our healers see her and assess her situation," replied the king. Roland tried to stand up but fell to the ground again; he hadn't slept well in months. Trying to protect his home and mother had taken everything he had. Alex made the healers attend to Roland and put him on a stretcher; he was asleep in mere seconds. The healers went to check on his mother next, and what they found was not good. Scarlett still wanted to see her sister. The healers tried to convince her otherwise, but she pushed past them; what awaited her was pure horror. Roland wasn't kidding when he said she was holding on, but it would have been merciful if he had put her out of her misery. Karen was mutilated by the disease; chunks of hair were all that was left on a head that was mostly covered in boils and blood-filled sores, some leaking green and yellow pus. Some were large pulsing blisters ready to pop. The whole left side of her nose looked like it had been chewed off and was covered in the same blisters and sores. Her teeth were all missing, and her jaw was only hanging on by a few tendons and bits of skin. Scarlett took the blanket covering her sister and pulled it off to shake and straighten it out, and that's when she noticed the disease didn't just mutilate her face, but also her body. Scarlett covered her back up and walked out. She ran to Alex with tears as her body shook with soft sobs muffling in his chest as he held her.

Alex asked Bromley, his head healer, what could be done. "Sire, in her condition, I'm surprised she's even still alive. She can't eat, and she is too far gone for any treatment we could offer her. It would be a mercy to let her go and take all the pain away." At this, Scarlett broke down and buried herself deeper in Alex's chest. He wrapped his arms tightly around her to support all of her weight and consoled her as much as he could. "Do what needs to be done, Bromley, but make it quick and painless." Bromley went into the small hut and did as he was bidden, as he had done many other times that day.

After ending Karen's suffering, the king ordered all the bodies to be taken to the sea and sent off in a Viking funeral. "Yes, sir, it will be done."

"Alex, what about Roland? We cannot leave him here alone. He has no one to watch after him; he's been through so much already, and his mother has just died." Scarlett said.

"What do you think we should do, sir?" Bromley asked. "We can't take in every child who has lost a parent; we'd have thousands of children in the castle. We have so much to do now just to rebuild our kingdom."

"HE'S NOT JUST ANY CHILD!! He's my family. He is all I have left now that my sister is dead. He is coming home with us; he will be ours now, and WE will adopt him. I think Mathias needs someone his own age around; besides, it will be good for both of them."

The king knew he wasn't going to change her mind and also knew she was right. Mathias did need someone his age to be around. Maybe it would bring him down from his high pedestal and make a change for the better within him. "Ok, Scar, we can take him in, but first we need to wake him up and let him say his goodbyes. Let him sleep until the other bodies are gathered on the carts, then we will wake him and break his heart with the news."

2

About an hour later, the sun was starting to get low in the sky, and Scarlett decided it was time to break the bad news to Roland before the sun set. She went to the young boy she would soon be calling son, and gently rubbed his shoulder until he regained a conscious state.

"Roland, wake up, dear. We need to talk."

"Ugh…. My queen…."

"Roland, you can call me Aunt Scarlett if you want. Listen, we need to talk."

"Where is my mother? Can the healers help her?"

"Roland…. your mother was too far gone, the plaguc had taken its toll, and she was in so much pain. We did what we could, but she didn't make it."

Roland jumped up and ran toward the hut he used to call home, but before he could get very far, Scarlett grabbed him and pulled him into her bosom, holding him tight as he fought to break free. He finally ran out of energy and just began to sob. He turned around, hugged Scarlett tightly, and cried into her shoulder, his tears soaking her chest. "You are coming home with us. King Alexander and I will raise you as ours. We have a son about your age, and he will be your new brother. We WILL take care of you. I swear it on my sister's life."

The king mounted his horse and rode over to his queen and newly adopted son, "Roland, you will ride with me. We

9

have much to talk about on the ride home, but first, go say your goodbyes and pay your respects to your mother. If there are any belongings, make sure to grab them now. I'm not sure when we will be out this far again. When you are done, make your way back to me, and we'll be off."

Roland didn't own much: he had the clothes on his back, which were torn to shreds, and his father's sword and sheath, which he decided to leave after Alexander had pinned him so swiftly. He took one last look around and gave his mother a kiss over the blanket covering her, said a prayer, and headed out to start his new life with his aunt and uncle, now his adoptive parents. He would also be gaining a brother from what he heard. He wasn't sure how he would fit in a castle as royalty. He was used to working and training, and helping his neighbors, not being waited on and served. He did look forward to new clothes and a real bed to sleep in. His mother had told him stories of the luxuries that the king and queen were accustomed to. Roland figured he was lucky to have this chance and would try to make the best of it.

"Are you ready, Roland?" Alexander asked.

"Yes, sir, I am," he replied.

"Roland, you don't have to call me sir; you can call me father, or if you're not comfortable with that, you can call me Alexander." Roland wasn't sure what to do, so he just shook his head. "Hop up here, son, we have a lot to talk about."

The two trotted along slowly. Alexander did this for a number of reasons. First, he wasn't sure how comfortable Roland was on a horse. Second, he wanted some time to talk to the boy before they returned to the castle. "First things first, no more trying to cut off my wife's head, I kind of like it where it is, and she's grown attached to it after all these years." He said with a light-hearted chuckle.

"I'm sorry I didn't……" Roland started to say, ashamed.

"I know you didn't. You were doing what you thought you needed to do to protect your mother," Alexander interrupted.

"Besides, I see raw talent that could be put to better use. You could hone it with a little more instruction and training. Maybe you could train with Mathias and my knights to clean up your style and take you to the next level. Who taught you to fight and handle a sword that way?"

Roland stayed silent for a minute, trying not to cry as he thought of his father, how much fun they had while they trained together. After a few seconds, he pushed the emotion away and spoke up. "My father and I trained a few days each week. We both had always hoped to work for you in the royal guard, but it was always just a dream of ours. We never figured we could be much more than farmers or blacksmiths like the rest of our family had been before us."

Alexander took a second to put his thoughts and words together, and then spoke softly to Roland. "Son….my wife, your aunt, now your mother, is royalty. She is more than a farmer or blacksmith. Your father should have come to us to try out to be one of our guards. But being a farmer and a blacksmith is just as honorable a position; without people like you, and all the others in our kingdom, no one would eat, no one would have weapons, and no one would be able to live."

"We were lucky," Roland said, "At least we were until the plague hit. We had enough food, time, and money to live well. We didn't get sick at first when we stayed to ourselves. But after a while, Dad became sick, so he distanced himself from us... He still brought us food and kept others away... kept the watch to keep us safe. After he was gone.... I was the only one left, and I thought Mom was safe. But then she, too, slowly got sick. When she got sick, I did what I could to keep her fed and safe. When word got around that it was just me protecting her, the villagers came around and tried to steal what little we had for themselves. At first, I felt bad for them. They were sick with open sores and gaping wounds, but my family... what I had left... needed to be protected. I used what my father taught me to dispatch them. Mom didn't do well for much longer, but I stayed to protect her."

Alexander was impressed with his will to live and the bravery he had to protect his family. That is what made him bond with Roland in the end; he was more like him than his own son. "Son, I will have you train with our guards if you so wish. There will be some other rules to follow. Same as the ones you have followed your whole life, be humble, be kind, and treat others, even the servants and maids, with respect. Treat your subjects with dignity and always protect those who need protection. Can you do that?" the King asked.

Roland thought for a second and said, "Respect and how I treat people won't be an issue, and I'm not sure how I'm going to handle servants and maids. Not that I won't treat them well, but I am not used to being waited on and served. I am used to cleaning up, working all day, and pulling my own weight."

Alexander smiled at this. His smile made him look years younger, and it was very contagious. Roland smiled back, feeling that this was how things should be. He was able to talk with someone and be happy, something he hadn't felt in quite a while. Alexander told Roland that he would be expected to pull his own weight when it came to training and his schooling, and helping out wasn't a bad thing, but it wasn't his job. His job was to learn to be a prince now. At that, the word prince, his jaw dropped. He hadn't thought of that until just now. He knew his mother was related to royalty, and after this pandemic, now he was going to live with the king, but the word "prince" never really entered his head.

"Prince? I'm no prince, I'm just an orphan you are taking in. I have no clue how to be a prince!"

The king laughed a full laugh and said, "Boy, you are no orphan, you are my son now. No one knows how to be royalty. Most are just born into it. And besides, Mathias will be there to help you along. Now, come, boy, we must get a move on and catch up to everyone. It's getting late, and there's more work to be done before we go home. "

Roland looked back one last time. His home was here. It was all he had ever known, and now the king—Alexander, his new father—was taking him away to a new home, an unfamiliar home. He was sure it would be easier in the castle and that he would be treated fairly and given anything he wanted, but it was new. Any boy his age would be scared. He would miss his home, his family, and his friends, but he would give this a chance. What other choice did he have?

3

As they neared the castle, Roland realized he had never been this close to the gigantic castle. All his life, he had only seen it from afar, from his lowly spot in the town. To him, the castle had always been just a statuesque monument that blocked out the sun in the morning. The actual size of it amazed him—He couldn't see the top of the castle from this angle, even if he craned his neck all the way back. He was astounded.

He also realized he had never seen the inside of the castle. The only homes he knew were his small home and the surrounding houses of mud, stone, or straw—or some mix of the three. The finest things he had ever seen were the colorful tapestries and paintings that hung in the town hall. He loved their vibrancy, so different from what he saw daily. Yet what greeted him now made everything he had ever known pale in comparison.

The tapestries of fine, woven silk that hung from the walls glimmered in the light. Deep reds and golden tassels danced before his eyes, mesmerizing him. Paintings, with their lifelike detail and depictions of women—some nude, in ways he had never seen—looked so real he blushed. Stained-glass windows sent reflections darting through every corridor, beams of colored light hitting his eyes and holding him captive, as though his life depended on following them.

Roland's astonishment showed on his face.

"What do you think of your new home?" Alexander asked.

Roland was at a loss for words. He could not wrap his head around it. It hadn't truly struck him yet that he would now be living so lavishly. "It's beautiful," he said, still amazed.

Alexander laughed low and heartily. "This is just the entry to the stables, my dear boy. Wait until you see the rest of the castle—and the Great Hall."

"I have heard stories of the Great Hall," Roland said, awestruck, "but I never dreamed I'd see it." He was still taking in all the new sights, sounds, and smells of his new home. It was such a contrast to the muted tans and browns of the dead grass, the mud that made their homes, the wheat they harvested, and the hay they used to feed their horses. Here, there were vibrant blues, shimmering blood reds, and gold and silver adornments—even in just the entrance of the castle that rose into the sky beyond sight.

Even the smell was different. He had thought royalty might smell different—and it did. He could smell horses and moss on the beams and stones of the vast building, but mingled with them were richer scents: tangy and fruity notes in the air, the radiant freshness of the grass outside, so unlike the dead grass at home. There was also the aroma of stews, soups, and meats cooking somewhere within, making his mouth water.

Alexander and his entourage led the horses down a long ramp into the underground stables. He instructed his healers to take the sick to the infirmary, to heal those they could, and to keep the others comfortable until their time came. The king rode to a larger stable where he kept his horse, a stall far finer than the rest and unlike anything Roland had ever seen.

Alexander slid from his horse, not a far drop given his enormous size, and lifted Roland down just as Scarlett rode into the stable, stopping beside the king. Alexander helped his wife dismount and set her down gently beside Roland.

Roland, still embarrassed that he had once tried to strike her, turned red and looked at the floor, ashamed.

"Roland," the queen said, her voice stern but soft, "look at me, son. Will you not meet my eyes because you are ashamed that you tried to hurt me, or is it because you dislike me? If it is the former, I hold no ill will toward you. You were protecting your mother... my sister."

Roland stayed silent for a few moments, then slowly looked up at her. "I'm sorry I swung at you. Yes, I was protecting her. But I promise never to try to hurt you again, my queen."

"Roland, now that we've taken you in, you do not have to call me queen. You may call me Scarlett—or even Mother, if you please."

"I don't know if I'm ready," Roland admitted softly, barely above a whisper, "but in time, I think I may be able to call you Mother and Father. Please don't be disappointed if I don't do it right away."

Alexander and Scarlett exchanged an awkward glance.

"Fair enough," the king said. "Now let us go to the Great Hall. We'll show you around your new home and introduce you to Mathias and all the servants."

He called a servant over and whispered instructions. The servant ran off.

"Roland, I've sent my servant for a new set of clothes for you. We should get you into something nicer—those torn clothes won't do."

"Servants?" Roland repeated. "That will take some getting used to. I've always done for myself, my family, and the people around us who needed help."

The thought that he would never again return to those people—or see his family—brought a tear to his eye, but he pushed it away, hoping he looked stronger than he felt.

The servant soon returned with the clothes and held up a red satin cloth so Roland could change behind it. He quickly changed into the new clothes.

"Come, boy, let's go," Alexander bellowed. "There's much to do."

He took Scarlett's hand and led her toward an old stony staircase, its steps damp with dew from the previous night's rain. Droplets slid slowly down the mossy stones, leaving trails behind them like snails.

Roland realized then that his life was about to change. He wasn't sure if it was for better or worse, only that it would take a great deal of getting used to.

Roland stared at all the different paintings and tapestries as they walked. Then, they came upon a huge room that stopped the young child in his tracks: The Great Hall. The Great Hall was a huge rectangular room in the middle of the castle with ceilings that seemed to go on forever. Large wooden beams stretched from one end to the other, dark browns and greys, and looked strong enough to hold heaven itself. There was an enormous fireplace in the center, made of stacked stones you could see from both sides, in shades of tan and brown. All handcrafted to look like huge puzzle pieces put together. The mantel that topped the firebox on both sides was massive—a dark red wood with unique carvings adorning it from end to end. Easily twenty-five feet long and two feet tall, the carvings were lifelike horses and castles, so rich and beautiful. The fire blazing within seemed to come from hell itself. It flickered back and forth like hundreds of snake tongues, mesmerizing the viewer and almost hypnotizing Roland. The firebox was vast and seemed boundless. Being in the middle of the room, you could see how massive it was. The blaze was so tall you couldn't make out anyone or anything on the opposite side. The logs stacked, for what seemed like a mile high, inside burned so bright they looked like molten metal, as though they might melt through the floor at any moment.

Throughout the hall, there were stained-glass windows, each with different patterns depicting the king, his queen, and the knights of the table. They twinkled in the firelight, sending beautiful, fragmented colors bouncing off the stone fireplace, forming ghostly figures. Above the fireplace hung stuffed animal heads. On one side, a large lion with ferocious teeth snarled as if ready to eat Roland alive, its mane large and ruffled. On the other side, a colossal elk with a broad set of antlers as wide as the fireplace stared down, its bright eyes gleaming and its coal-colored nose glinting in the low light. Between the windows were a variety of birds—pheasants and quail with rich, dark feathers in every color. Some appeared as if in flight, others perched gracefully as though waiting to be fed. The most impressive of all the hunts was something Roland had never seen, only heard about: a rhino. In all its glory, its massive head hung above Alexander's throne. Its armor-like skin was thick and strong, grey as the ash from the blacksmith's shop. Two horns crowned its head—one large and battle-worn, the other smaller and rounded yet just as deadly. Its small black pearl eyes glared into the vast room, the deep wrinkles beneath them showing its age but lending it a strange beauty. Roland was in awestruck.

On each side of the fireplace sat gigantic tables made of ironwood, dark and beautiful, with long grains running lengthwise. Deep craters with knots near the ends of each board. Each table could easily hold a hundred people or more. Above each table hung fine woven tapestries with the king's family crest sewn into them. The tapestries were dark blood-red, edged in stone grey, with golden tassels hanging from the bottoms. Between them hung large iron chandeliers, suspended from the same beams by thick chains, each holding twenty-five candles. Yet even they paled in comparison to the light of the great fire. The floors were smooth stone of a kind Roland had never seen before. A light grey with long, veiny strands of black running through them. To him, it was the most beautiful thing—

coming from huts with dirt floors, this was beyond anything he could have imagined.

Attending to each table, Roland observed four young women and one big, burly man beginning to place food upon them. Alexander placed a hand on Roland's back and led him toward the group. The king first introduced him to Hax, the cook of the castle.

Hax was exactly what Roland imagined when he heard "the king's cook." He was a man of considerable girth, as tall as he was wide, with thick brown muttonchops following the line of his large jowls. His long, wavy hair looked as though it hadn't been washed in months—if not years—and hung just past his thick neck. His face was pale as ash, with tight, suspicious black eyes like those of a crow. A short, flat nose with wide nostrils, like that of a pig, sat heavily upon his face. Truly, he was an odd-looking man. He wore what looked like a potato sack tunic, covered by a greasy, white apron stained every color of the rainbow, with scarcely an inch left clean. His trousers were just as filthy, bunched around his waist, and tied at the ankles. Like most servants of the time, his feet were only covered by thin cloth wrappings. They were worn through, his long, sharp toenails poking out, yellow and green, looking infected and oozing. Roland shivered at the thought that Hax might touch his feet before cooking. The thought sent a chill up his spine.

Hax looked at the boy, then at the king. "Aftanoon majesty, hope your ventcha' was fruitful. May I ask if the boy is heeya to join the kitchen staff?" he said with a slight drawl and accent the boy hadn't heard before. Hax eyed him and looked him up and down suspiciously. "He seems kinda' scrawny to be pullin' bags a taters and such, an' he perty dirty ma' lord."

Alexander let out a hearty laugh loud enough to surprise Hax, who stumbled back a few steps. "No, Hax, this young man is of royal blood. He is Scarlett's nephew." All of the good cheer drained out of the king's face as quickly as it came as he said, "The boy's parents died in the plague, so we are taking him in. His name is Roland, and he is now to be considered our prince, same as Mathias." Hax and the young women shared a look of understanding that Roland had yet to understand. He didn't know that they were already aware of Mathias's displeasure over a new person being brought home and called a prince. Another person who would take the time of others, in essence, take them away from Mathias's beck and call. Roland would learn this in time. Hax figured that within a week, Mathias would have him broken down, if not in the infirmary.

"Hax, if the boy needs anything, you make sure he gets it, and make sure you sit him near us at the great table for tonight's feast, understood?"

"Yes, majesty. I'll make sure to fatten him up. No prince in this castle will be skin and bones if I have a say so." That made the boy smile. He was hungry and hadn't remembered the last time he had anything substantial to eat. He wondered what type of food royalty ate. He had heard Hax bring up "taters," and he loved the potato soup his mother used to make. The thought of his mother pulled at his heartstrings again, but he wanted to keep his composure; there would be plenty of time to mourn later on. "Son, if you need anything, you needn't hesitate to ask any of these women or Hax; they are here to serve you. Don't disrespect them; they are our workers, but if you treat them right, they will do the same. Now let's be on our way, there's much more to see and many more people to meet."

4

Alexander and Scarlett walked him around the castle, up and down many levels. The entire castle was extravagant and over the top, unlike anything he had ever seen, with fine silks and linens, clean silver utensils, and dinnerware. It was warm and clean. They introduced him to many more servants, a few knights, and, to his delight, a few children. There were more people in the castle than there had been in the village while he was growing up. "Ok, Roland, a few more things, and we can slow down and rest. I'm sure this is a lot to take in. I want you to meet my advisor, whom some call a magician. His name is Seoul. Some people are scared of him, but he is my most trusted confidant."

Seoul was exactly what he had imagined from the stories he had heard in the village. He was very tall and made the enormous king look small. He was twig-thin, but you could only tell by the size of his wrists that stuck out past the flowing blue sleeves on his magnificent robes. The robe was a rich dark blue with gold, Celtic knots adorning the ends of the sleeves, the hood, and the neckline. It made him seem larger than life. His beard was white as freshly fallen snow and went well past his chest, almost to the middle of what Roland supposed was his stomach. His nose was tall and square; at the bridge, it looked as though it dropped off. His hair was just as white as his beard, but with strands of grey sprinkled throughout. It stood up at the end, frazzled all over his head, with no rhyme or reason to the way they went. Seoul's skin was a yellowish grey, riddled with areas of brownish spots on his hands, face, and neck. They were what his parents called sun spots, but the man looked as though he had not seen the sun in months, if not years. The thing Roland noticed the most was the man's piercing eyes. They were a very bright blue, but the pupil looked like the night sky, as if holding an entire galaxy within. When you gazed into them, it was as though you could see everything past, present, and future. It was hard for him to look away.

"Seoul," the king said loudly and boisterously, purposely dragging his name out. They broke away from the stare. "How are you, my friend?"

"My king, I see you have returned. I came back with the healers. I saw to it that everyone who came back made it to the infirmary safely and have been seeing to it that the ones who can be saved will survive. I also see you have returned with the boy. I am glad to see that Scarlett's nephew will be joining us." The king looked at the wizard curiously. "How?"

The wizard returned his gaze to the boy, then to his king. "I see much, my king. I have foretold another child for you and the queen. The way that it happened was not revealed to me. I saw the vision of the queen's sister losing her life to the plague, but I did not see her child in that vision. I deduced that this was him. His future looks very bright just from the aura that surrounds him." Roland was surprised. He hadn't thought much about his future. His main purpose in life over the last few years was surviving and protecting his family, mainly his mother.

Roland spoke up for the first time, in a meek voice, "Have you seen my future, sir?"

"Roland, I see many things, but to tell them may change your destiny, and by changing one's may endanger everyone who surrounds you. All I will say is that you have a good aura about you, and I expect great things from you. Have you thought about your future? You have many new opportunities now that you are in the castle and the king's son."

"I haven't thought much about it, but my father and I always talked about joining the royal guard. I thought that I would be a farmer all of my life, maybe a cattle owner at best."

"Well then, my boy, the King should take you to see Arthur and Gary Robert; they are in the courtyard training the knights and the recruits. I think young Mathias may be there also. He usually 'trains' with them," he said with a slight tinge in his voice.

Seoul knew of the stories of Mathias and his personal "magician," who was with the young prince more often than not. Megendra was not what Seoul would consider a good influence, for he knew how to influence the prince's decisions for his own advantage. The knights didn't like to train with Mathias and hated putting recruits in with him, but knew there'd be issues if they didn't. They would say 'they were damned if they did and damned if they didn't.'

Finally, Alexander said, "Let's head down to the training arena. I will introduce you to more of the men and Mathias. I'm sure he would be happy to have another boy his age in the castle, another friend, since he doesn't have many. I think most of the boys and the girls are intimidated by him." Alexander knew deep down why his son had no friends. He heard the rumors in the royal hall of his son's entitlement over people he considered lesser because they weren't of royal blood. So unpredictable was his temper that even the slightest hint of embarrassment would end in merciless revenge. "Accidents," he called them. Then, there were the rumors of him groping and assaulting the women for his own sick pleasure. But no one dared complain to him or his advisors, and so he played the ignorance-is-bliss card, knowing full well that anyone who came forward would face his son's wrath. He wanted to think he had raised his son better than the rumors floating around him. Though deep down, he knew the truth, but chose to ignore it. Not knowing that this would be his downfall.

As they walked to the arena, Roland again noticed the vastness of the castle, the craftsmanship of the linens, and the intricate carvings in the stone—artistry like he had never seen. It was all so overwhelming. As the three of them crested the slight incline of the grounds, Roland noticed the huge marble-carved pillars that opened up to a long set of steps leading down to the stone courtyard and arena. At the bottom of the steps, the entire area was made of perfectly carved stones set into the ground in a giant circular pattern, surrounded by carved wooden statues of the three former kings and the current king. The training arena was enclosed by a wall of large black stones set so perfectly that from above it looked like a beautiful charcoal painting. Again, he was overwhelmed. As they descended the steps, he saw the weapon racks come into view, filled with the most unique and well-crafted swords, maces, spears, and axes of all kinds. He had never seen such quality weapons before—certainly nothing like those in his village.

Alexander could see the wonder in Roland's eyes and asked, "What do you think?"

Roland was speechless for a few seconds before softly uttering, "It's amazing! I've never seen anything like this before, not even in my dreams."

"Well, son, I can't make dreams come true, but I will do my best to make sure you have what you need."

As Roland walked up to the beautiful training area, he noticed a young man facing off against what was obviously one of the guards. The young man, he assumed, was the prince—he had heard much about him but had never actually seen him in the villages. The prince was a thin boy with golden-blonde hair and a nose that slanted like a mountain slope, slightly bent to the left side. His bright blue eyes looked straight through you, yet there was something in them that unsettled Roland. He wasn't sure what it was, but it sent a chill down his spine.

5

Mathias stood in an aggressive stance, holding two axes that looked decorative but also deadly. The weapons were intricately carved with snakes and filigree on the handles, their sharpened blades gleaming with a lethal edge—not something one would expect in a training session. In an instant, the onlookers watched the young prince charge at the royal guardsman, Thomas. Thomas was one of the most experienced and loyal knights. As Mathias ran, he leapt and swung both axes down at Thomas, who easily evaded the attack. Twisting to his right, Thomas used the flat of his blade to hook the boy's ankle as he landed, tripping him. Mathias fell face-first into the dirty stone. Clearly embarrassed and enraged, the future king's fiery eyes revealed his anger as he got up.

"A full-fledged attack isn't always the answer, boy," Thomas explained. "You are too aggressive and need to learn defense. Muscle and speed will not always win the day."

This only made Mathias more irate. Again, he bombarded the knight, and again Thomas dodged. This time, as Mathias passed him, Thomas grabbed his gorget and swung him around, slamming him into the ground near the edge of the horse area and knocking the wind from him. The child's face turned fiery red. He was no longer thinking straight, tired of losing. Most men usually let him win, but on this day, Thomas wasn't in the mood—especially after hearing how the boy had spoken to the staff earlier in the day while his parents were away in the village.

Mad as ever, Mathias grabbed a handful of horse dung and threw it at Thomas just as the knight was about to offer another lesson. It hit him in the face, and while Thomas was surprised and distracted, the furious prince went for a death blow. He charged at the knight, leapt into the air, and bore down with both of his lethal axes.

Before the king or any spectators could react, Seoul conjured a wind spell and cast it at the boy. A hurricane-force wind blew Mathias into a nearby cart full of rotten vegetables meant for animal feed. A ghostly chain appeared from thin air, wrapped around him, picked him up, and lowered him to the ground, tightening until he could not move.

Alexander wasn't sure what to think—it all happened so fast. The boy screamed and cursed, humiliated, struggling to free himself. Before the king could speak, the chains exploded into dust. In the background, Megendra moved his hand in an eerie motion—he had freed his prince. Mathias sprang up, adopting a ferocious stance, ready to attack again, drool and spittle hanging from the edge of his mouth like a feral beast.

Alexander finally spoke when he noticed Megendra and Seoul staring ominously at one another. "ENOUGH! EVERYONE, CALM DOWN!" His voice boomed across the arena, sending birds fleeing from the trees. "Mathias, what are you doing? You know this is just training! We don't try to injure or kill anyone—especially our own."

"Father, he was cheating and trying to embarrass me! He doesn't deserve to be a knight—he's no more than a peasant!"

"ENOUGH, I said! You are done. Go to the castle and relax. This isn't how you are supposed to act. You are a prince, start acting like one. As for Thomas being a peasant, he is one of the most respected and best knights and trainers we have. You should be thanking him for training you."

Mathias curled his lip at the thought of thanking someone he considered beneath him. "Fine. I will go to my quarters."

"Before you go, you need to meet Roland. He is your cousin. His parents died in the plague, and he will be living with us. You are to treat him as a brother—maybe help him train and show him around once you calm down."

Mathias looked Roland up and down, then sneered. "I don't have time to entertain peasants. I have more important things to do. Come, Megendra, let us leave these… people."

"MATHIAS!" The king's boisterous voice resonated through the grounds. "This isn't a request—it's an order. You will show him around, and you will treat him with respect. You will treat him as a brother. He will be living with us from now on—we are taking him in as our own."

"I will do no such thing! He has no royal blood or right to be here. He is a hayseed barbarian from outside the castle walls!"

Alexander's face turned red. He strode toward Mathias at a pace surprisingly fast for a man his size. The boy cowered, knowing he had angered his father. At heart, he was a coward, and most of the castle knew it.

"YOU WILL DO AS I SAY! I AM YOUR KING, BUT MORE IMPORTANTLY, I AM YOUR FATHER!!"

Roland could not imagine the wrath Alexander's foes must feel when his anger was in full force. The man was huge—a force to be reckoned with.

"Fine, Father," Mathias said, his tone passive-aggressive. "I will summon him tomorrow and 'show' him around." He walked past Roland with a smug look, shoulder-checking him as he and Megendra passed.

"Come, Roland," Alexander said, sensing how awkward the exchange had been for him. "Let me show you around the rest of the grounds."

6

Roland lingered by the weapons rack, admiring the artistry of the weapons in the armory. They were unlike anything he had seen in the village—the carvings, the engravings, the blacksmithing were second to none. He picked up one of the swords and felt its perfect balance, the care that had gone into forging it, sharpening it, and oiling it. He could feel the power in it. Holding it, he felt powerful.

Thomas had watched Roland as he admired the swords and as he picked one up. He was curious about the boy. He yelled over, "Boy, what do you think of our armament? I see you've picked out one of our claymore swords. How does it feel?" Roland was so lost in his amazement at the sword that he only snapped out of it at the end of Thomas's question. He quickly recovered, turned to the knight, and said, "Excuse me, sir, I'm sorry, but I missed your question."

Thomas laughed and answered, "It's ok, boy. I saw you admiring our weaponry, and see you've taken to the claymore. Do you have any training?"

Before Roland could answer, Alexander spoke up. "He has no formal training, but he almost took the queen's head off. He has spirit," he said with a slight chuckle. He added the chuckle only because he saw the shame in Roland's eyes when he mentioned the attack on the queen. "But that's in the past."

Roland explained how his father had shown him how to use a sword—not a claymore, but a more common sword. His father had always wanted to be part of the royal guard and had practiced with Roland in case he ever got the chance. When the plague hit and villagers started looting and robbing, his minimal training helped—especially after his father died.

Thomas took a moment to take everything in and said, "Well, let's see what you've got. I'd pick something a little more lightweight to start and work your way up to the claymore. What do you think?"

Roland picked up what was known as a knightly sword. It was lighter and easier to handle for a boy of his size and strength, and he put the claymore back. He made circles with it in front of him, getting a feel for it the way his father had taught him. Roland walked up to Thomas and put himself in the stance he had learned back in the village.

Thomas smiled. "That's a good stance to start with, but plant your back leg and make sure your grip is tight."

Roland did as he was told, strengthening his stance. Once he did, Thomas came at him—not full force, but enough to wake Roland up and get his adrenaline going. Roland was mostly taught offense against would-be attackers, so muscle memory took over, and he hacked and slashed at his trainer with no restraint. He was quickly and easily disarmed.

Thomas laughed. "You children seem to only care about attacking, but defense is just as important and, in most cases, will save your life."

Roland picked up his sword and apologized for his reaction. "Can we try again?"

Thomas wasn't sure it was a good idea, but he gave in. "I will be a little rougher this time, so be ready." With the speed of a hungry cat, he leapt at the boy.

Roland went on the defensive, guarding against every hack, jab, and slash that came at him. He was backed up and fell more than once, but kept getting up, throwing in a few jabs and slashes whenever he saw an opening. He was learning to dance around the attacks, starting to see a pattern in Thomas's moves—or at least he thought he did. When he felt he had spotted the pattern, he tried to disarm the man. But on a dime, Thomas changed his moves and disarmed the boy instead.

Out of breath and obviously tired, Roland dropped to a knee, trying to steady himself. Once he was able to get up again, he said with a little laugh, "I'm ready for more."

Thomas gave a short laugh. "I think that's enough for today. But I'm fairly impressed. With a little training, you could be good, maybe better than good, with time. For now, you need a good meal in you and some rest. We can pick this up again in a few days. You need to get acclimated to this place first. There is a lot to get used to around here."

Roland and the king headed back toward the castle. Alexander went on about battles he and Thomas had won and lost, but all Roland could think about was more training.

7

Roland was excited at the prospect of real instruction. Yet with that thought came a pang of shame, as though he were saying his father's training wasn't enough. Gods, he missed his parents. The thought of them being gone brought a tear to his eye.

When they reached the castle, Roland saw Mathias standing next to the gate with his mother. The look on his face was one of defiance and anger; Roland could see it clearly.

At the gate, Roland bowed to the queen and the prince. Scarlett was about to introduce the two when Mathias cut in. "Ahh, the street rat again."

Scarlett, clearly shocked, didn't know what to say. Alexander stepped in after seeing the look on his queen's face. "MATHIAS, watch your tongue! Interrupting your mother is rude, and this 'street rat,' as you call him, is family. He will be staying with us from here on out. Maybe you can be nice and have at least one friend in the palace… and even learn a few things from him."

The young prince laughed at his father's statement. "What could I learn from him? I'm already a great fighter, I'm respected and feared, educated, and the future king. What could he teach me?!"

His father and mother both answered simultaneously, "Manners and empathy."

Mathias's face twisted with outrage, but he said nothing. The silence stretched until Roland broke it, locking eyes with the prince. "It's a pleasure to meet you. I saw you training in the courtyard. Maybe someday you can give me some pointers?"

Mathias said nothing for a few moments, then replied with malice in his voice, "I don't think you're in my league quite yet. But maybe if I knock you down enough, you might learn from that and move past the first-year trainees."

Roland knew he was trying to get a rise out of him, but it wasn't working, which only made Mathias angrier. "Maybe you're correct, Prince Mathias. I've only had minimal training outside the castle."

Scarlett spoke up. "Son, can you show your 'new' brother around the castle?"

"New brother?! We have servants for that—this is below me!" Mathias nearly screamed.

The king stepped in again. "You'll do as you're told!"

Mathias saw the look in his father's eyes and knew better than to protest further. "Yes, Father," he said, his voice dripping with contempt. Then, with a low snort, he added, "As you wish."

"Come with me," he grumbled at Roland.

Roland looked at his new parents and decided it would be best to follow Mathias.

The young prince did the bare minimum to show Roland around—walking from one room to another, mumbling what each area was at a brisk pace, his flowing crimson and gold cape trailing behind him. Roland struggled to keep up. They passed through the kitchen, where the prince muttered something about a cook named Hax, then into the great hall and the trophy room. Here, Mathias slowed just enough to gloat over the many trophies he claimed as his own. Roland, having seen the prince fight during training and knowing his attitude, suspected most of those trophies weren't earned fairly—but he kept that to himself.

8

Mathias finally slowed when they reached his room, and Roland braced for another round of boasting. The large oak doors before them were inlaid with gold, silver, and precious stones Roland had never seen before. Inside, a young girl, not much older than Roland, was cleaning. Mathias began talking about the size of his room and his trinkets, but his words trailed off when he noticed the girl.

The brunette froze, clearly surprised to see both boys walk in. Her face was streaked with dirt, her dark brown hair tied into pigtails beneath a shawl, and her green eyes stood out against her grimy clothes. Sweat already dotted her brow, but the surprise made her flush as red as a fresh apple. After a moment, she regained her composure and curtseyed.

"Sorry, lord. I was just finishing the cleaning. I'll be on my way," she said nervously.

Roland wondered how the prince would behave—he remembered his cruelty on the training grounds. Mathias' demeanor shifted instantly. He stood straighter, his usual scowl melting into a grin that carried something darker beneath it.

"What is your name, sweet girl? Are you new to the castle?" he asked slyly.

35

Taking a deep breath, she replied, "No, my prince. We have met before. My family has been serving the king for a few years now. My name is Amadalia, daughter of Guinevere." Her voice carried a note of unease.

Mathias drifted closer, running his pale fingers down her face, making her visibly uncomfortable. In a timid voice, she said, "I will be going now, I am finished. I need to get to the next room."

As she tried to leave, the prince grabbed her arm roughly. "Where are you going? Stay awhile. I'm sure Roland wants to get going," he said, throwing Roland a wicked glance. At the same time, Amadalia shot Roland a panicked look, fear in her eyes.

Thinking quickly, Roland said, "Prince Mathias, you've had a long day. You must be tired. Instead of showing me the rest of the castle and my room, why don't you rest and let the young servant woman finish showing me around?"

Mathias' face flushed red with anger, his glare sharp and foul. Before he could respond, Amadalia sprinted to Roland's side.

"FINE!" the prince barked. "Both of you—GET OUT!"

They didn't hesitate. The moment they crossed the threshold, the heavy wooden doors slammed shut behind them. Roland and Amadalia exchanged a quiet chuckle, careful not to let the prince hear.

They walked down the hall toward the next room she was assigned to clean. The castle was so vast that each room was separated by long stretches of corridor. Their next stop was Gary Roberts' room—the man Roland had met earlier in the arena. Mathias, Roland noticed, kept well away from the servants' quarters.

"Thank you," Amadalia said first.

Roland smiled. "You looked uncomfortable, so I figured I'd step in."

"It's not the first time this has happened," she admitted. "He has touched me in ways I didn't like, and tried to undress me. Each time it's gotten worse. I feared this time might… go too far. I'm not the first girl this has happened to—some have left, some have disappeared, and some have… well, they aren't around anymore." Her voice faltered, and a tear slipped down her cheek, carving a clean line through the dirt.

"Well, now," Roland said, "I'll have to find my way around the rest of the castle myself, Miss Amadalia."

She laughed lightly. "You can call me Ami," she said, blushing.

"Alright, Ami. If you need anything, just let me know. I guess I'll go explore this 'new home' of mine."

"WAIT!" she blurted, then immediately looked mortified, her face reddening again. In a softer tone, she said, "The least I can do is show you to your room."

"You know where I'm staying?" Roland asked, puzzled.

Ami's face lit up. "Oh, everyone knows everything about you already. The king sent one of his fastest riders back to prepare for your arrival. You've been the talk of the castle all afternoon."

Roland felt his cheeks warm.

"You're kind of a big deal," she teased with a chuckle.

He felt awkward. He wasn't used to this kind of attention—he'd always been on the side of the peasants, a nobody, not someone who drew whispers in the halls. Ami must have sensed his discomfort. She placed a hand on his shoulder.

"Are you alright? Did I say something wrong? I didn't mean to offend you."

Roland shook his head. "No, please, don't take it that way. This is just new to me. I'm not used to this kind of attention. I grew up differently—it feels… foreign."

Ami looked down. "I've spent most of my life here. I'm not royalty, but I've never known life outside these walls as you do. I may be a servant, but I know I have it better than most—and we were sheltered from the worst of the plague."

"I'm sorry," Roland said. "I didn't mean to make you feel ashamed, or make this all about me."

"It's alright, I didn't take it that way," she reassured him. "I just don't want you to feel different. My life isn't like yours, and I haven't had it too rough. I just think we have a lot in common, and I want you to feel like you can talk to me if things get too serious. Some of those royal meetings can get… pretty stuffy. I barely understand a word they're saying most of the time." She smirked slightly.

"Let me show you to your room—it's only a few doors down," she added.

Roland perked up. "That sounds like a good idea. I can explore later—I'm exhausted. I'm sure I'll get lost a few times before I remember where to go."

Ami laughed. "I know it will happen. I'll keep a lookout and help you when I can. Let's go."

Ami led him down the hall to his room. From the outside, it was plain compared to Mathias' room—an arched oak door with wrought-iron handles. He opened it, and the inside was just as plain as the door, but still a huge step up from what he was used to. There was a bed like he had never seen before, and a chest at the foot of it. He opened the chest and found blankets and more clothes—clothes that weren't tattered or patched together from scraps.

"What do you think? I cleaned your room myself."

Roland looked around and realized it was the cleanest room he'd ever had.

"It's very nice. You did a great job—thank you."

Ami blushed. "Well, I'd better get back to cleaning. I'm a little behind as it is. I'll be seeing you around."

Roland met her eyes. He noticed how pretty they were and started to blush, but caught himself. "I'm looking forward to it."

Now it was Ami's turn to blush. She smiled, turned, and walked out, shutting the door behind her with a loud clunk. Roland lay down on the bed and realized how comfortable it was. Maybe he could get used to this.

As he lay there in his thoughts, he drifted off without realizing it, not truly aware of how tired he was. His dreams mixed nightmares of his mother with dreams of Ami. He slept long and hard until—

9

A knock at his door woke him. For a moment, he wasn't sure where he was, but then it all came flooding back. He got up, wiped the sleep from his eyes, and answered. One of the maids stood there, letting him know dinner would be served soon. She handed him another change of clothes and instructed him to go to the bathing room before dinner.

Roland set the clothes on his bed, then turned back to the woman. "Excuse me, ma'am—what is your name?"

"My name is Emily, Lord. I'm head of cleaning in the castle."

Roland didn't think he'd ever get used to being called "Lord or prince," so he asked her to call him Roland, at least when they weren't in front of royalty. She agreed.

"Emily, I'm still getting used to the castle. Which way is the bathing room?"

"It's four doors down on the left. Take the hallway, and it will be the first on the right. You'll see the steam and smell the tallow and sap… Roland." She gave him a wayward smile, a touch of color in her cheeks.

Roland thanked her as she turned to leave. He picked up his clothes—and then heard footsteps. Thinking Emily had forgotten something, he turned, only to jump as Mathias slammed the door and rushed at him with a small hatchet in hand. The prince shoved Roland against the wall, pressing the blade under his Adam's apple. Roland dropped his new clothes.

Roland could feel the heat from where it had just been sharpened, and the damp residue of the whetstone. He also noticed the prince hadn't done the best job sharpening it—but it was still deadly.

Mathias' pale face was dark red with rage, his body trembling, giving the goosebumps on Roland's neck an unpleasant shave, drawing a small drop of blood. His voice came out in a broken half-whisper, half-yell, strained and spitting.

"Who do you think you are—embarrassing me in front of the servants?! They're mine! I can do what I want to them, when I want, however the hell I want! I am the future king! They are MY property—they obey MY orders! You just got here, and you'd better learn your place, or you'll end up like everyone else who crosses me!"

Roland saw an opening, knocked the hatchet from Mathias's hand, and used a move his father had taught him called a hammerlock. He twisted the prince's arm behind his back and forced it upward—just enough pressure to keep him from moving without causing injury.

Mathias was surprised at how fast and agile Roland was—but the audacity of this "trash" to lay hands on him burned worse than the pain.

"Take your hands off me, or else I'll—"

"Do what?" Roland cut in. "Tell your father? He already knows how you are. Once I show him the mark you left on me, I'm sure he'll believe me. Or maybe you'll try to get back at me? Right now, that doesn't seem like much of a threat. If you want to hurt me, do it in the training arena. At least then you'll have an excuse, if you win."

The prince laughed, then twisted wrong and winced in pain. "IF I hurt you. I will destroy you—you've seen what I can do!"

Roland laughed in return. "From where you are right now, I doubt it. And yes, I've seen you in action—you cheated. I've heard the stories already. Your anger could be an asset, but you let it blind you."

Mathias winced as he chuckled. "There are no rules in war. A peasant like you should know that. From what I've heard, if you fought like me, your parents would still be alive."

The vile smirk on his face hit its mark. Roland's grip faltered just long enough for Mathias to wrench free.

Now defenseless, the prince kept his guard up, disgusted that Roland had bested him at all. How the hell did a dog from the bottom of the kingdom get the better of me? He thought. He's stronger and faster than I gave him credit for. I should get out before he has another chance.

Roland's face twisted in disgust, but he kept his composure. "You are an evil little bastard, Mathias."

"Again—there are no rules in war, brother of mine," Mathias said with disdain.

"What the HELL do you mean, war?! Training isn't war—we aren't at war! What is wrong with you?" Roland shouted.

"You know nothing of being royalty," Mathias spat. "Life is war. You win, or you lose—and I don't lose. No rules. No mercy. I do what I want and take what I want because I am the future king!"

Roland was speechless. He couldn't understand how someone with such good parents, born into wealth, power, and a certain future as king, could think this way. How did the King and Queen not see it?

"The people of this kingdom will not stand to have a king like you, especially after your father. He's loving, gracious, and fair."

Mathias laughed. "My father is weak. The people should bow to him. I will be an overlord. Any who stand against me will perish. With the royal army at my side, I'll march through other kingdoms and take them for myself."

Roland shook his head. "Get out."

He kicked the hatchet toward him, watching as Mathias picked it up, opened the door, and left—never turning his back to Roland.

Roland sat for a moment, thinking maybe the village would have been a better place for him. After calming down, he got up, picked his clothes back up, and made his way to the bathing room.

Roland knew where the room was by the smell Emily had described to him. He had never bathed anywhere but the river near his village and had only heard his mother's stories about the tallow and sap the royals used to clean themselves.

As he entered, he was amazed. The room was massive, with all the window openings draped in rich red silk, giving it a sensual, almost decadent feel. A large fire pit burned in the center, with metal buckets hanging above it to warm the water. Steam curled through the air. Scantily clad women stood at metal basins, washing men and women alike, pouring hot water over them. Candles glowing everywhere, casting a hedonistic, low light.

The smells were new to him—sharp enough to sting his nose and eyes, though not unpleasant. It was sensory overload, something he had never seen before and would never forget.

A tall, striking redhead woman approached and looked him over, noting his open mouth and cheeks as red as autumn apples.

"You must be the new Lord, Roland. There's been a lot of talk about you."

Roland couldn't stop staring. She reached down and gently pushed his mouth closed.

"My name is Eden. Come with me. You were supposed to go to the next door down. This is the adults' bathing room."

Roland remained frozen, still gazing around at the women, until Eden grabbed him by the ear.

"Come on, let's go," she said, dragging him through a small door connected to the beautiful chamber.

The next room was for the younger set, and it was nowhere near as grand as the adults' room. Older women, fully clothed, worked there, and burlap covered the windows. The smell was different—less sultry but still warmed by a firepit and lit by candles. Here, the women scrubbed the younger bathers roughly, unlike the gentle rubbing and massaging he had seen before.

Eden noticed his disappointment.

"In a few years, I'll see you in the other room. You're old enough to wash yourself, but if you need anything, ask Agnus—she'll help you." She pointed to a woman near the firepit.

Roland thought Agnus looked like an old witch. Thin whitish-grey hair, a crooked, wart-covered nose, and teeth either missing or stained deep yellow and black. He looked back at Eden and thanked her. She walked away, and he made his way to Agnus to see which bath was his. She handed him a bar of something and pointed toward a nearby tub.

She filled it with warm water and told him it was ready. Roland thanked her, climbed in, and began washing.

He had never had a warm bath before. The bar of cleaner made his skin feel smoother than ever, and he realized he had never felt this clean or this good. It was something he could get used to. After the run-in with Mathias, the bath eased some of his tension.

When he finished, Agnus handed him a robe and showed him where to get dressed. The clothes Emily gave him earlier were clean, good-smelling, well-fitted, and colorful instead of the torn hides and mismatched fabrics he was used to. The colors felt a bit much for him, but he figured he'd get used to that, too.

He stood before a mirror, studying himself—something he rarely had the chance to do. His village had none, except when the magnates came down to the local shops, carrying mirrors on their belts or pulling them from their purses to show off. They hadn't come around since the first mention of the plague.

Agnus came up behind him, handed him a comb, and asked when he last had a haircut. He shrugged. His mother had cut his hair last, long before she got sick. Roland tried to tame his hair as best he could. Agnus noticed a small cut on his neck with a drop of blood trickling down and dabbed it with a cloth from her apron.

"Are you all right, lord? Do you want me to have the nurses put something on it?" she asked.

He paused. "No, I should be fine. Thank you, though."

"Okay, lord. You should be headed to the dining room. Your first one is important—don't let the—" she lowered her voice—"little twit get to you. He can be… something else."

Roland rolled his eyes. "I know."

After a moment, he asked shyly, "Can you point me to the dining room?"

She gave him directions, and he set off toward his first royal dinner.

10

As Roland neared, the smells from the kitchen hit him full in the face, making his mouth water. He hadn't had a hot meal in a long time. Lately, he'd survived on whatever he could scavenge, and only occasionally trapped a bird or squirrel.

Passing by the kitchen, he spotted Hax and the other cooks working frantically to prepare the feast. He caught sight of turkey, chicken, pheasants, deer, and boar. Behind them were puddings, cakes, and tarts. His stomach growled, and he quickened his pace toward the dining room.

When the hallway opened into it, he was stunned. The room was enormous and elegant, its windows adorned with silk, its walls hung with tapestries depicting the adventures of past kings, ending with King Alexander. The artwork was breathtaking.

Then he saw the table—sixteen feet long, six feet wide, supported by six massive legs carved into lions. Intricate patterns and shapes ran along the edges. The surface gleamed a golden hue in the moonlight streaming through the windows, and even the chandelier's glow made it shine.

He was wonderstruck.

As he entered the great room, Roland saw the king and queen being seated.

"HELLO, YOUNG MASTER," Alexander bellowed loudly.

As Roland moved closer to the table, Alexander lowered his voice to a reasonable volume.

"Sit, my young prince. Tell us about your day. You look much better now that you've had an afternoon in the castle."

Roland was taken aback at being called "prince," just as he had been by most of the events since arriving at the castle.

"Prince?" he said, sounding perplexed.

Alexander looked at him as though he didn't understand. Scarlett spoke up after a few seconds.

"Well, yes, my son. We have brought you in as our own—that makes you a prince… our prince."

Just as Roland was about to respond, Mathias walked in and said, "He's no better than a bastard son! He isn't of royal blood—he is NOT a prince! I am the prince, the only heir."

Queen Scarlet's tone held a touch of sternness.

"Yes, Mathias, you are the heir. But Roland is now your brother, and you will treat him as such. He has royal blood—the blood of my sister runs through his veins—which means he has royalty in him."

Mathias started to protest, but his father gave him a look warning him to go no further. He sat down heavily, making his discontent plain.

"So, Roland, how have things been?" the king asked.

Mathias shot a look at Roland, clearly anxious about whether he would mention their earlier "disagreement." Roland caught the look but paid it no mind.

"It was good. It was nice to meet a few people, bathe, and get a few hours of restful sleep. I'm looking forward to a good meal—it's been a long while since I've eaten a real one."

Alexander laughed boisterously again.

"There is plenty to eat and plenty to drink. Fill your belly to your heart's content—that's what it's there for, my boy," the king said, taking another huge swig from his large auroch horn and wooden stein.

The stein caught Roland's eye. It looked large enough to hold half a barrel of mead and was made of what appeared to be beautifully grained kingwood, rare in the kingdom and something Roland had only ever seen in drawings. The auroch's horn was marbled black and white, and the whole stein glistened with mead dripping from it.

Alexander noticed Roland eyeing the cup and roared to Hax, "HAX, bring the boy a stein of mead," his words clearly on the verge of slurring.

Scarlett interjected, "He's still young—he shouldn't be having mead."

When Hax arrived, Alexander waved him closer, poured most of his drink into his own cup, and told him to give the rest to Roland.

"Be careful, boy—it's strong."

Roland took a large sip and almost immediately spat it out, but managed to choke some down. The king and queen laughed loudly, and Hax joined in. Roland turned red.

Through his laughter, Alexander said, "I told you it's strong. It's also an acquired taste. The cup is yours to keep, lad. Hax—wash his cup out and get him and Mathias some milk."

The rest of dinner went without incident, aside from a few scowls from Roland's new "brother" whenever he made their "parents" laugh. Roland couldn't remember the last time he'd laughed so much or eaten so well. He ate until it hurt, realizing how much better his life was going to become.

He still felt a pang of guilt that his own family wasn't there to enjoy it, but he knew they would be happy to see him safe, with a better life in the castle among his extended family. He decided then and there to make the best of it— train hard, make both his new and deceased parents proud, and help the less fortunate in the kingdom's villages.

Roland was growing tired despite his nap earlier. Scarlett noticed and told the boys it was time to turn in. Mathias, as usual, protested. Roland rose from his chair and began gathering his plates, but Mathias laughed.

"The peasant thinks he's a servant, cleaning his own place," he said, snorting like a pig.

Roland didn't understand and gave a confused look.

Alexander spoke up. "Son,"—clearly irritating Mathias by calling another boy that—"we have servants to do that for us. They work in exchange for room and board. Leave it for the kitchen stewards. Mathias, instead of acting like a jester, you'd do better to help Roland learn our ways."

Mathias grunted in disapproval and left the table without another word.

"Sorry, I'm not used to all this yet," Roland said.

"Don't be sorry, son. This is all new—you'll learn soon enough," the king replied.

Roland walked over to Scarlett, hugged her, and thanked both her and Alexander.

"Thank you both for everything today, and especially for taking me in. I know it's probably not easy for anyone to bring someone new in and teach them the ins and outs of your lifestyle. Thank you, and I love you both. I'll prove taking me in was worth it."

Both looked bewildered but touched. They weren't used to such heartfelt gratitude. It tugged at their heartstrings.

Alexander stood, pulled Roland into his massive arms in a slightly painful embrace, and said, "Son, you have already made us proud. We know you'll do great things. We love you."

Roland smiled warmly at them and headed toward his room.

Once in the hallway, he spotted Mathias lurking in the shadows.

"That was some good bootlicking out there," the prince said coldly, stepping into the dim light. Roland tensed. Mathias toyed with a small poignard dagger—its mahogany hilt engraved with intricate designs and topped with a large green jewel set in gold. The blade gleamed in the candlelight.

"My parents are soft, charitable, and compassionate," Mathias sneered. "The way they treat servants and peasants is disgusting. The way they're treating you is sickening. Once the novelty wears off, they'll treat you like the rest. Still nice—but nothing like now. You'll just be a peasant in a castle. Leave now and avoid the heartbreak."

Roland may have been young and naïve, but he knew what he was doing.

"Thanks for the concern, but I think I'll stay," he said with a slight smirk.

It made Mathias furious.

"When I'm king, you and all the swine in this castle will be treated as such. I will not be soft on anyone—especially you!"

Roland quipped as he walked away, "Well, luckily our parents are young and healthy."

Mathias hated that Roland was quick-witted.

"You think you're clever—you've been warned," Mathias said.

"Thanks," Roland replied sarcastically and walked away.

Roland got back to his room, still stuffed from dinner and still in a good mood, even after the meeting with his new brother. Just to be on the safe side, he locked his door. He noticed his bed was made, a few pairs of fresh clothes and boots were neatly placed on his coffer, and the room had been tidied up. It made him think fondly of Ami, the sweet girl he'd met earlier.

After sitting for a few minutes to reflect on his day, Roland decided he'd get a few hours of sleep so he could be up early and head down to the arena to start training. Pulling back the blanket, he lay down and thought about how lucky he was—here in a warm bed, with new parents who loved him despite what Mathias had said, and with a full belly. With thoughts of that and Ami in his mind, he drifted into a deep sleep.

11

The next morning, he awoke just before sunrise. He'd slept better than he had in a long time, only waking a few times due to dreams he now couldn't remember. He couldn't believe how much energy he had. Grabbing a set of clothes, he dressed quickly, put on his new boots, and headed to the training arena.

On the way, he spotted Eden, Hax, and Ami, most likely getting things started for the day. He waved as he ran past them. Hax and Eden gave halfhearted waves, but Ami waved back excitedly. As Roland neared the front gate, he slowed down, captivated by the sight of the rising sun shining through the stained-glass window.

The sunrise alone was beautiful—hues of pink and purple streaking across the sky—but as the light fractured through the glass, hundreds of colors and shapes danced across the floor and walls. It was one of the most beautiful things he had ever seen.

Lost in the kaleidoscope of colors, Roland didn't notice Thomas emerging from Eden's room. The knight approached quietly and placed a hand on Roland's shoulder, startling him and triggering his defensive instincts. Roland tried to use the arm bar on Thomas, but the older man easily brushed it off and had Roland in an arm bar of his own in seconds.

"Whoa, boy—calm down," Thomas said, a hint of glee in his voice and a smile on his face.

Roland, realizing who it was, apologized and knelt down in front of him.

"On your feet, boy, I'm not going to hurt you. Nice try, but I've got a few years of experience on you."

Roland, beet red, apologized again. "Sorry, sir, I'm just a little on edge. I was in such a trance from the light I didn't hear you coming."

Thomas chuckled. "Your reaction time was pretty quick."

Roland smirked.

"Yes, this is a beautiful place first thing in the morning," Thomas continued. "Where are you headed so early?"

"Actually, I was on my way to the arena. I want to start my training as soon as possible," Roland replied, perking up.

Thomas looked surprised. "Well, that's nice. The prince had to be dragged down some days, or he wouldn't get up until lunch. It's good to see some initiative. You're in luck—I'm heading there myself."

The two set off toward the training grounds. The walk wasn't far, but it was enough time for some small talk. Thomas decided to see if Roland's story about why he wanted to train would stay the same.

"My father always wanted to be in the royal guard, and he trained with me. I took a liking to it and thought it would be a good way to honor him," Roland said.

Thomas smiled. "Well, we'll see how you take to our training. If you're good enough when you come of age—and if the king allows it—you might join. From what I've seen so far, you might have a future in this."

Roland was happy to hear it.

Just then, they reached the arena gates. "Do you still want to train with the claymore you had your hands on yesterday?" Thomas asked.

Roland paused. "What do you suggest, since I'm just starting out?"

"Well, normally I'd have trainees start with our wooden swords to assess skill level," Thomas said after a moment's thought. "But I've seen yours. For now, I'll start you with a knightly sword. Years ago, a sailor ended up on our shores with what he called a 'Viking' sword. We've adjusted and modified it for our use—it's a great sword to learn with."

Roland went over to the rack and started looking at the ones Thomas pointed to. He studied them, picked one up, and turned it over in his hands, examining the markings, the shine of the blade in the morning sun, and the engravings on the hilt. He shifted it between his hands, feeling the weight and grip, and gave it a few light practice swings. He knew this would be a good starter weapon. Eventually, he wanted to learn them all.

Thomas watched him closely. The boy was taking this choice seriously. "Is that the one you've decided on, Roland?"

Roland gave it one last look. "Yes, I think this is the one."

"Alright then, boy—let's get started."

12

And so began what would be a long, prosperous journey. Roland's first real training session with Thomas was exciting, educational, and painful. He applied the pointers from his first day, closing the gaps in his stance. Thomas was most impressed by his restraint—when Thomas spotted a flaw, he'd knock Roland down or smack him with the flat of his sword. Roland would get back up, adjust, and keep going. He never lost his temper and almost never made the same mistake twice… almost.

As the days went on, Roland's defense and offense both improved. His swings became smoother and more precise, his blocks faster, almost as if he could read the next move before it happened. Thomas couldn't have asked for a better student.

Roland's dedication was such that he began to wear Thomas out. To keep things fresh—and try to tire the boy out—Thomas rotated in his best knights. Roland adapted quickly, making only a few mistakes before correcting them. Eventually, even the most experienced knights were worn out by him.

So Thomas raised the challenge—two knights at a time. At first, this threw Roland off both mentally and physically. But after two weeks of grueling practice and plenty of mistakes, he could fight two men at once with near-flawless execution.

Thomas was astounded and proud. He knew Roland's dream of joining the Royal Guard would one day come true. After just three and a half months, the boy was already as skilled as some students who had been training for years.

13

After a few months of training, Alexander brought it up at dinner one night.

"How goes the training, my boy?" the king asked in a spirited voice. It was obvious he had started in on the mead early; turkey juice dripped down his chin onto his stomach.

Roland looked up with a big smile.

"It's going well. Thomas says I'm further ahead than most of the students he's had."

Hearing that, Mathias laughed and said, "He must have forgotten how fast I learned. I promise you aren't further ahead than me," he added maliciously.

Scarlett, not wanting a fight to break out, quickly interjected.

"Mathias, you've been training years longer than young Roland. I'm sure your brother is going at a good pace, just as you did."

Of course, Mathias hated Roland being called his brother, but he had been disciplined enough to keep those thoughts to himself.

Roland, feeling a little arrogant and annoyed with Mathias, spoke up.

"He told me my training… that I had in the village… helped immensely," he said with a sarcastic smile, carefully avoiding saying "my father" so as not to hurt the king's feelings.

Mathias laughed like a lunatic.

"A bunch of untrained farmer peasants know nothing of swordsmanship," he said between laughs.

Roland kept his smile and looked directly at him.

"Well, why don't you come down and show me what I'm missing? Try to teach me a few things. I haven't seen you at the arena since I arrived. Maybe you need to come down and shake the rust off with me?"

Mathias could see Roland was trying to get under his skin, but he wouldn't let him—at least not at first.

"You're not ready for me," he said dryly. "You may never be."

Roland let out a small laugh under his breath and said just loud enough for the prince to hear, "That's what I thought."

That did it. Mathias slammed his chair back and stood up violently.

"Okay, peasant!" he screamed. "I'll meet you down there in three days—a full four months since you got here to train. We'll see how good you are!" Spit flew from his mouth as he yelled.

Not hearing Roland's quiet jab, the king and queen were startled by the outburst. The king, clearly tipsy, laughed heartily, while the queen stood and barked, "SIT DOWN! What is wrong with you?!"

Still fuming, Mathias shouted, "I'm tired of this peasant coming in here thinking he's at the same level as me. He is nothing! I AM THE FUTURE KING! He should be bowing to me, on his knees!"

"For someone who THINKS he is the future king, you are acting like a tyrant the people would overthrow. You have a lot to learn before your father or I allow you to be king!"

Enraged, Mathias screamed at his mother, "ALLOWED?! I am the prince—it's my birthright—"

He stopped abruptly as a tight grip on his shoulder forced him to his knees. His father, still sober enough to grasp the seriousness of the boy's behavior, lifted him off the ground by that shoulder and slammed him against the cold, wet stone wall.

Mathias saw the look in his father's eyes and knew he had crossed a line.

"I don't know who you think you are, or if you've forgotten who you're talking to," the king said in a low, firm voice. Mathias could smell the rancid turkey on his father's breath, and droplets of food and mead spit flecked his face and beard.

"It will be over my dead body that I leave my kingdom— the one I have spent my life building—to you if you plan on acting like this. You have a lot to learn and need to be humbled before you're anywhere near ready. The people in this kingdom are good, hardworking folk who treat us well, keep our home clean, our bellies full, and our land plentiful. You'd be wise to learn that sooner rather than later."

He lowered Mathias to the ground but kept his hand on his shoulder.

"Who would you have take over then?" the prince asked, his tone less defiant but still edged with pain. "Him?!" He pointed at Roland with a shaking finger.

Roland looked up, surprised the prince would even suggest such a thing.

"At this point, he would be the better choice," the king said flatly.

Mathias's temper flared again, but before he could speak, his father's grip tightened. One look from the king, and the rage drained into reluctant submission.

Feeling defeated, Mathias said the words he knew his father wanted to hear.

"You are right. I have a lot to learn before I can be king."

With a hard swallow, he turned to his mother and Roland.

"Mother. Brother. I am sorry for my words and actions."

The king released him. Scarlett, still upset, said, "Dinner is done. Both of you are excused." She took her goblet of wine, hooked her arm through her husband's, and began walking away.

"I am going to bed," she said.

"Goodnight, Mother," both boys replied.

Once they were out of sight, Mathias shot Roland a dark look.

"Three days from now, I will show you pain as you've never felt. There is no way I will let you be king. This kingdom is mine."

Roland looked baffled.

"I don't want to be king. I didn't ask for any of this."

"Then leave," Mathias growled, keeping his voice low to avoid another round of his father's wrath. "If not, I'll make certain you have no chance to be anything more than the farmhand swine you were before they took you in like a wounded bird."

"I'm not leaving," Roland said quietly, almost to himself.

"Your funeral, brother," Mathias replied coldly before stomping off to his bedroom.

Roland, wary of an ambush in the dark, slipped a dinner knife into his pocket and took a roll for later. After a few minutes, he headed to his own room, locking the door tightly. He placed the knife near his bed and decided to get some rest, especially if he was to continue training the next day.

He fell asleep almost immediately and once again dreamed nightmares that faded upon waking.

14

The next morning, Roland met Thomas at the arena, as usual beating him there. If Roland hadn't arrived first, Thomas would have been worried.

"Good morning, Thomas. How are you this morning?" Roland asked.

Thomas let out a big yawn. "Tired."

"Are you alright?" Roland asked sympathetically.

Thomas smirked. "I'll be fine—just a little more exercise than I planned last night."

Roland looked confused, then remembered seeing Thomas leave Eden's room more than once over the last few months.

"Oh," he said shyly, blushing.

Seeing Roland's discomfort, Thomas changed the subject quickly. "Why don't we get started?"

"Can I talk to you about something?" Roland asked.

Thomas looked at him curiously. Normally, Roland couldn't wait to begin training, but now he looked troubled.

"Of course you can," Thomas replied.

"So…" Roland recounted the events of the night before, admitting that his derisive comments may have escalated the situation. He explained that Mathias had challenged him under the guise of "teaching" when, in reality, it was to embarrass—and most likely hurt—him. The fact that his father had pinned him against the wall and scolded him only made matters worse.

Thomas took it all in for a moment before speaking. "What Mathias did doesn't surprise me. He has a temper and is very entitled. You saw his outburst with us in training on your first day. In war, there are no rules, but in training, there are. He has injured students and trainers alike so often that most of the time, we just let him win. People who have embarrassed him or refused to fall in line have disappeared in the past.

With the argument that ensued last night, I'd be willing to say he wants to make you disappear—but Megendra has counseled him and told him you are too 'high profile.' So my guess is, he's out to seriously injure you… maybe even kill you."

Roland had already suspected as much. "Well, I guess I'd better train harder if I plan on staying alive," he said with a melancholy look.

Thomas gave a half-smile. "Funny part is, Mathias hasn't been down here much lately—he thinks he's beyond my training. But after the last three and a half months, you are far beyond him in skill and knowledge of swordsmanship. The issue is: how will he retaliate when you defeat him in the arena? Or how will he cheat to get at you?"

Roland considered this for a few seconds. "I guess I'll have to keep it close so his ego isn't destroyed—but I won't let him win. If I do, he'll keep acting the way he does. His ego will stay overinflated. He might be the future king, but he isn't now, and I won't bow down to him."

"My best advice," Thomas replied, "is to go meet with Seoul and seek his counsel. If you haven't spent any time with him, I suggest you do. He can be a great ally. Also… well, all the knights and I have something for you."

Roland perked up. What could they possibly have for him? What had he done to deserve anything from noble men like these?

"Come with me," Thomas said, prompting the boy to follow.

They headed toward the small blacksmith hut a short way from the arena. Roland had seen the blacksmith, Horace, in there sharpening weapons, and had once spoken to him about sword-making.

"Horace, do you have the piece I commissioned?" Thomas asked.

"Yes, sir," Horace replied, stepping out of a cloud of steam. The steam was red from the molten metal in the forge, glowing like embers dancing in a burning forest. It looked like the early morning sunrise just before the light overtakes the dark—an eerie yet beautiful sight.

The hut smelled of hot metal and an acrid tang from the fires burning so hot. Horace's face was covered in soot and fire scale, making him look as though he wore war paint like some of the natives on the far side of the island. He was dressed in a heavy-duty tan leather apron, large black gloves, and a long-sleeved cowhide shirt. His boots looked two sizes too big for his small frame.

The parts of his face that weren't blackened showed old burn scars. He had no hair, and Roland assumed from the scars on his head that it had been burned off. His round face and bulbous nose made Roland think he might actually be a dwarf, like in the stories his parents had told him.

Horace went to one of his many workbenches and rooted through it until he uncovered a large black walnut box, beautifully stained to show the long, tight grain. On the back were two thick iron hinges; on the front, a small, delicate iron latch. Horace hobbled over and handed it to Thomas.

"Thank you, Horace," Thomas said, passing the man a small leather pouch full of—Roland assumed—gold.

"My pleasure," Horace rasped. "It's one of my best pieces, and it was a joy to make something special instead of the typical swords and spears I usually forge. The hilt I'm especially proud of. I hope the young master likes it."

The light in Horace's shop was dim, so Thomas led Roland outside. A small table stood against the building, and Thomas laid the box on it. As he opened it, the sunlight reflected off the contents, momentarily blinding the young boy.

When Roland's eyes adjusted, he saw a beautiful sword—not just any sword, but a custom-made masterpiece. He looked at Thomas, then back at the sword, then at Thomas again.

"Is this for me?" he asked, his voice cracking.

"Of course it is," Thomas replied. "You've been one of the best students we've ever had—easy to work with, humble, even though you're one of the youngest and best. Don't let that go to your head. We had this made for you. We were going to wait a bit, but with your battle in three weeks, I decided to give it to you now so you can get used to it."

Roland held back tears. He had never been given such a gift.

"I can't accept this," he murmured. "I'm not worthy of it."

Thomas laughed. "Too bad, my friend—it's yours. If we didn't think you deserved it, we wouldn't have had it made. This is a lifetime sword, not one pulled off the rack."

Roland humbly picked up the sword. Its blade was slightly longer than his practice sword. The edges were razor-sharp, and the steel bore a distinctive pattern of banding and mottling—reminiscent of flowing water, almost like a rose pattern. Between the twisting designs, the bare metal shone like a mirror. A long blood groove down the center carried a blue hue that reminded him of the ocean, shifting fluidly when viewed from different angles.

The crossguard matched the hue of the blood groove, silver-blue, gleaming in the morning light. Roland could see why Horace had been so proud of the hilt. The handle was made of rosewood, a premium material with excellent durability, rich color, and a fragrant scent—rare in the kingdom. Its grain was exquisite, with long strands alternating from dark to light, almost mirroring the blade's own patterns. It fit his hand perfectly, feeling as though it belonged there.

The pommel was made of a thin piece of metal that matched the blade and was set with a rare ocean-blue Paraiba tourmaline stone, the final touch to this extraordinary weapon.

"I can't use this sword," Roland said timidly. "It's a piece of art that should be hung in the great hall."

"The sword will last as long as you take care of it," Thomas said. "The process the blacksmith used makes it one of the strongest swords in the kingdom. Only the king and I have ones made the same way. And, just so you know, the materials for the hilt and pommel were given to me by King Alexander himself. Try it out—how does it feel?"

Roland lifted the weapon fully out of the box, amazed at how light it was. It moved fluidly, each swing smooth and effortless.

"It feels right," Roland said. "Like it was made for my hand."

He took a few swings, dancing around as if surrounded by invisible enemies.

"Can you feel how light it is?" Thomas asked. "Horace designed it for balance, reach, versatility—and, of course, beauty. A one-of-a-kind sword, made to win battles."

Thomas grabbed a belt. It had a shoulder strap with a scabbard attached, as well as a sheath on the belt itself. Though not as fine as the sword, the belt was made of durable black leather.

"Try it on," Thomas said, handing it to him.

Roland passed the sword back to Thomas, adjusted the straps, and settled the belt and shoulder strap in place, wiggling to get them to sit right.

"How does it look?" Roland asked.

Thomas handed the sword back. As Roland sheathed it, Thomas smiled proudly. "Like a young knight, ready to defend the king—or win any battle put before him. Now, let's go try out the sword. You're already late enough for your lesson today." He laughed, and they headed back to the arena to train.

15

When the day's training ended, Roland returned to the castle. He went to the bathing room, greeting Agnus as he entered and again as he left. Once clean and dressed, he found Ami. After some small talk, he asked, "Can you show me where Seoul's sanctum is?"

"Oh no," Ami replied softly. "I won't go down there. I'll take you to the stairs, but I'm too scared to go any farther. The noises and lights that come from there… they frighten me."

Roland saw the fear in her eyes. "That's good enough," he said gently, touching her hand. She blushed. Realizing what he'd done, he quickly pulled his hand back, his face turning red.

Ami clasped her hands together, rocking side to side with a sweet smile. "Okay, let's go before I'm late to help clean up for dinner."

She surprised him by taking his hand and leading him to the far side of the castle. At the staircase, she pointed down. "He's down there." Again, Roland could see the fear in her eyes.

He bowed. "Thank you, Ami."

As he looked up, she leaned forward and kissed his cheek, then ran back toward the kitchen. Roland touched the spot where she had kissed him, feeling a warm rush. He paused for a moment, then turned and began the long descent down the stairs.

The stairway was shadowy, lit only by a few candles. As he descended, the walls grew colder, carrying a strong, mildewy smell mixed with other scents he couldn't identify. His best guess was that potions and their ingredients had permeated the air. The walk seemed to last forever. The sounds he heard and the dim flashes of light didn't frighten him, but he could see why they might scare Ami.

Just when he thought the stairs would never end, a faint glimmer appeared ahead. As he drew closer, he realized the light was seeping through the cracks of a large wooden and iron door, its surface carved with countless inscriptions and runes.

"Come in, Roland," a low, deep, breathy voice called from behind the door.

Cautiously, Roland stepped forward and pushed it open. The loud creak made him jump. Inside was a sight unlike anything he had imagined—neither his wildest dreams nor his worst nightmares compared.

The heat hit him like a wall, dizzying after the chill of the stairwell. The dark grey stone walls were the same as those on the stairs, though here many were covered with a green, moss-like substance. In the center of the room blazed a large fire pit, built from strange stone and mud.

On either side of the pit stood two old ironwood tables, arranged in a V-shape. They were scarred and battered—chunks missing, burn marks, and stained surfaces where they weren't covered with objects.

On the left table lay two large books bound in what looked disturbingly like tanned human skin, the yellowed surface stretched tight around the stitching. A human skull, white as a summer cloud, rested on top. Another book of the same material lay nearby, its pages covered in unfamiliar words and pictures. The fragile sheets, yellow and brown, reminded him of dead autumn leaves.

The right table held several colored glass tubes and vials, each filled with liquids of varying hues. The firelight cast sinister shadows over them. Large mortars and pestles sat nearby, containing mixtures of plants and liquids—he recognized only one: nightshade.

Near the window stood Seoul. Roland had glimpsed him briefly when he first arrived at the castle, but had been too preoccupied to remember much. Now, he saw the tall man more clearly. He had long white hair, though his true build was hidden beneath a cloak. He was feeding a hawk perched to the left of the window.

As Roland entered, the hawk roused, puffing its chest and fixing him with a sharp gaze.

"Seoul, sir," Roland said respectfully, though timidly, "may I have your counsel?"

When the wizard turned, Roland's pulse quickened. For all he knew, the man might strike him down with lightning or turn him into a frog. His expression was unreadable.

His black cloak seemed to float as he moved, its hem sweeping past his feet, a large hood hanging down the back. He looked Roland up and down.

"Welcome, young man. I was wondering when you would come meet me," he said in a rich baritone.

"What brings you here? What counsel do you seek?"

Seoul extended his arm, and the hawk hopped onto it, waiting to be fed and stroked.

"Well… I don't know where to start," Roland admitted.

"The beginning is usually best," Seoul replied with a grin, showing crooked but surprisingly white teeth. "Sit, and we'll talk about what troubles you."

That eased Roland's nerves. "There was a fight—or really, an argument—with Mathias about who's better in the arena. He's afraid I'll try to take his throne when the king dies. Things got out of hand."

Seoul stroked the hawk's head. "Mathias is not fit to be king—at least not with the entitlement he has now. The company he keeps only feeds his ego. His short temper has caused problems, too. I'm sure you've heard the rumors about how he deals with disobedience and perceived threats?"

Roland nodded.

"The ones who've disappeared, even I—with all my mystical powers—cannot find. I suspect Megendra's involvement. So, what do you need from me?"

Roland took a breath. "He's offered to 'help' train me, but it felt more like a challenge. Thomas warned me that if I embarrass the prince, he'll seek retribution or try to kill me in the arena. I'm willing to keep the fight close, but I don't intend to lose. If I do, his ego will only grow worse. I need your opinion on how to handle this."

Seoul snapped his arm, and the hawk flew back to its perch.

"It sounds like you've already decided to accept his 'help.' And yes—if you beat him, he may retaliate, especially if you humiliate him. My advice: give it everything you have. Perhaps knocking his ego down will do some good. He may turn to Megendra to make you disappear, but I will ensure that doesn't happen. I would also invite the King and Queen to watch your progress. With enough witnesses, he might restrain himself—though there's no guarantee. Are you certain you can defeat him without injuring him so badly you seem like a savage?"

Roland considered his words. "I think I can. I'm good at holding back—unlike him, I don't let emotions cloud my judgment. I'll work with Thomas to plan."

Seoul's lips curved into a faint smile. "I'll be there. Megendra will be too—he protects the prince because he benefits from him. The boy behaves as he does because of that influence. I will see that the match is fair."

"I appreciate that, and the time you've given me today. I hope that if I need more counsel from you, I will be welcomed," Roland said.

"I think we will have a long history together in the end. You are always welcome," the man replied as he stood up.

The hawk flew back to its master's arm and eyed Roland.

"Don't be afraid, young one. He is not dangerous unless you tell him to be; he is just another tool. One day, I will teach you how to use him as one."

The bird lowered its head and stretched toward the boy. Roland reached out slowly with his hand and stroked the hawk's head. The bird lifted his head, pushing Roland's hand toward his chest. As Roland pulled back, the hawk shook out its feathers and flew back to its perch.

"What is his name?" Roland asked curiously.

"Hierax. He showed up here shortly before you. He is the only one of his kind in the kingdom. I think he was lost from his kettle and came here. I found him down by the water, tired and lost. He took to me very quickly. He hasn't been friendly with anyone else except you."

This made Roland smile.

"Thank you again for everything. I should go now—I have a few days to train so I can do my best."

The wizard nodded, and Roland turned and made his way up the stairway.

When Roland walked out of the stairway door, Ami was waiting nearby.

"How was it? Did he turn you into a frog or show you your future?!?!"

Roland laughed. "No, nothing like that. We talked, and he gave me sound advice."

Ami had a sullen look on her face. "Oh, I thought you would have something exciting happen."

He laughed at this.

"I'm done with my duties for the night," she said sheepishly.

Roland, taking the hint, replied, "Let me walk you to your room."

The girl blushed and said, "Okay."

As they took the short walk, he started to tell her about Hierax the hawk. Unbeknownst to them, as they went into the servants' hall, Mathias was hiding in the shadows, brooding, watching the two pass by. He was clenching his teeth, balling his fists, conspiring and plotting against the boy he thought of as a threat. He walked out of the depths of the shadows and headed off to his room.

On the other end of the castle, Roland dropped off Ami and headed toward his own room. Once inside, he sat on his bed, taking a deep breath before letting out a long sigh. It had been a long day with much to think about. After a few minutes, he lay down and slept, dreaming again of the future—dreams he would always forget upon waking.

<h1 style="text-align:center">16</h1>

The next morning, Roland accidentally overslept. Although it was only fifteen minutes or so, it was a big deal to him. Once he was dressed, he raced down to the arena. For the first time, he did not arrive before his mentor.

Thomas, however, obviously did not care. He simply asked, "Are you alright?"

"Yeah, I'm not sure what happened. All I remember is having the oddest dream, but as usual, it escapes me now."

"Well, are you ready to resume your lessons?" Thomas asked.

Roland explained the conversation he had with Seoul, repeating the wizard's counsel.

"I've decided to give it all I have, but I need to know how to make it look like I'm just sparring, while still embarrassing him—like you do to me when I make a mistake. I can strike him with the flat of my sword on his side, or take his feet out from under him."

Thomas looked concerned. "Are you not worried about him trying to kill you if you embarrass him? You know how he can be. He may not be a greatly skilled fighter, but what he has learned, we taught him. What he lacks in skill, he makes up for with his devious nature and his anger. You have seen him throw mud in our faces when we have him cornered."

Roland leaned against the fence, thinking about it. "I think I can handle him. Seoul will be there, and I think he would intervene if he thought Mathias was going to kill me. But there's no guarantee."

Thomas put his hand on the boy's shoulder. "Then I guess we should get started. You don't have long until the battle, and we need to get you used to the new sword."

The two went into the arena, and over the next three days, they trained hard. Roland took to his new weapon immediately. It was balanced so well and flowed so freely, like it was an extension of his own arm. Thomas and the other trainers taught him the best ways to 'spar' against the prince—how to trip him up, how to use Mathias' anger and emotions to force him into mistakes.

They also did their normal training, brushing up on small errors. Roland started off going one-on-one, then two-on-one, and finally three-on-one. Everyone was again amazed at the speed the boy exuded and how quickly he absorbed his training.

Arthur decided to add a lesson on what Mathias might try in order to blind him and gain an advantage.

"It's human nature to swat at anything coming toward your face. Whether it's a cloth or a stone, it will at the very least make you back up, lose focus, or, at worst, blind you. In your training, we don't do that. The prince most likely will. So I'll show you some ways to combat it, or at least deflect it."

17

The night before the boys were to have their sparring match, the whole family sat together at the dinner table. After the meal was finished, but before dessert was served, Roland spoke up.

"Father, Mother… Mathias and I will be sparring tomorrow. I hope that as you watch, you can take notes and tell me where I've gone wrong and how I can improve. I would like you to be in attendance so I can prove I haven't been wasting my time since I've been here."

Mathias smirked and let out a small laugh. "I didn't think you would agree to spar with me—especially since I have so much more experience. I figured you would back out," the young prince bragged.

The king and queen exchanged a look and smiled.

"I'm glad to see that you two are finally getting along," Scarlett said, beaming with a half-intoxicated smile.

Alexander, also smiling and clearly inebriated, raised his voice. "Boys, we are going to make a spectacle of this! HAX!" he bellowed toward the kitchen.

Hax waddled in, his large belly swaying from side to side. "Yessum, sir?"

The king shouted, spittle flying from his mouth, "Spread the word to everyone in the castle and the upper village that it is mandatory to attend the arena at the sixth hour, to watch our boys spar! Let them see how our future king and prince will defend the kingdom!"

Hax turned to shuffle away and muttered another "Yessum, sir," before disappearing into the kitchen, already calling for others to spread the news.

Roland looked stunned and uneasy. Mathias noticed and leaned in smugly.

"You weren't expecting an audience, were you? Don't worry, I'll take it easy on you. I wouldn't want to embarrass you in front of the entire kingdom."

Roland kept his composure. "Thank you, brother. I look forward to learning from your experience."

Mathias was about to respond when Hax stumbled back through the doors carrying dessert. He held a tray piled high with sliced apples, pears, berries, honey, and nuts. Ami followed behind with another tray, laden with sweet pies, tarts, and custards spiced with cinnamon, nutmeg, and saffron. The aroma made Roland's mouth water, distracting him from his quarrel with Mathias.

He reminded himself not to overindulge, with so much riding on the next day. Carefully, he took just one tart and a few pear slices drizzled with honey and sprinkled with cinnamon. Mathias, on the other hand, loaded his plate with a bit of everything.

When Roland finished, he asked to be excused. He rose, bowed to the table, and said his goodnights.

"Sleep tight, brother. Tomorrow will be an… experience," Mathias said, his voice thick with contentment.

Roland met his eyes squarely. "Yes, yes, it will. I'll see you then."

As he turned to leave, he caught a glimpse of something disturbed and unhinged in the prince's gaze. The look unsettled him. Mathias was unstable and willing to fight dirty—especially when cornered. Roland hoped his training had been enough.

Once in his chamber, he locked the door, climbed into bed, and checked to make sure his knife was close at hand. Just in case.

18

Roland rose early the next morning, both nervous and excited for what lay ahead. After washing and dressing, he went to the kitchen, grabbed a small piece of bread from Hax to settle his stomach, and made his way to the arena.

He stopped by the weapons shed to retrieve his sword and sheath.

Thomas was already there, sharpening the training swords along with his own.

Roland approached casually and asked with a hint of sarcasm, "Are you ready for today?"

Thomas chuckled and smiled. "The real question is, are you ready?"

Roland sat beside him and began sharpening his own blade. "I'm as ready as I'll ever be. But if he wins, he'll be impossible to deal with. At least toward me. And he'll only grow crueler with the women here in the castle. I've already caught him trying to defile one. He wasn't too happy when I stopped him."

Thomas raised a brow at this. He knew Mathias was cruel, but not to the point of rape. The boy was getting bolder with age. His voice took on a tone harsher than Roland had ever heard from him.

"Then you cannot lose today."

Roland caught the seriousness in his tone and looked away. He wasn't offended or threatened, but he understood the weight of what Thomas meant. He inspected the edge of his sword one last time, then sheathed it.

"Now I need to figure out what to do before the competition," he muttered in a detached voice.

Thomas stood beside him. "Have you ever meditated before?"

Roland looked at him curiously.

"Come with me. I'll show you. It will calm both body and mind. Let's find a peaceful spot."

The two walked past the stables and into an open field, where a single massive tree stood: an ancient horse chestnut, its age unknown. It was the only tree outside the forest, a sentinel watching over the plain.

Its thick trunk was covered in gray bark, while the rest was a deep, rich brown, heavily furrowed with age. Its leaves, though not in bloom, hung in light green clusters—thin, oblong, veined, with coarse serrated edges, drooping from the branches like weary hands. In season, Roland had often enjoyed its roasted nuts, though not today.

"Let's sit under this tree," Thomas said. "It's as good a place as any. Meditation is about focusing—or emptying—your mind. It's a mental and physical discipline. I meditate to relax, reduce stress, and focus on what lies ahead. Eden and I meditate every morning."

Roland smirked, amused.

Thomas caught it immediately. "Focus, boy! Sit comfortably on the grass. Close your eyes. Breathe deeply—in… and out. Try to clear your mind. If it wanders, bring it back to your breathing. Once you've stilled your thoughts, remain there. Then, notice the sounds around you. Feel the grass beneath you. Pay attention to your thoughts and emotions. And when you are ready, open your eyes slowly."

He gestured for Roland to try.

The boy sat loosely cross-legged, lowered his head, and closed his eyes. He did as his trainer had instructed. Roland felt his mind clear, and after a few minutes, he opened his eyes. What he saw in front of him frightened him. He was no longer in the field under the tree. Thomas' face wasn't there. He opened his eyes into the near future.

19

He was in the castle, in the middle of a bloody battle. Many of the royal guard were lying dead in the main hall, blood pooling all around them and splattered across the surrounding walls. Young men wearing chain mail over their gambeson jackets and black leather gloves were attacking the remaining royal guards, pressing toward the king.

His father, the king, looked older, frailer, with large tufts of grey hair hanging from his head and beard. Leading the attackers was a man with dirty blonde hair, wielding twin axes. A guard rushed at him from behind with his claymore, but the blonde enemy turned, easily disarmed the man, and slit his throat with both axes, spraying blood everywhere.

Roland saw the enemy's face and swore it was Mathias—but older. It cannot be, he thought. There's no way he would go this far.

"What the hell is going on?" Roland roared.

The man he took for Mathias raised his axe toward the king, and as the swing came down for the king's head, Roland screamed in horror, "NO!!!"

Roland's head snapped up, and he woke back in the field under the tree. He was sweaty, and tears gathered at the corners of his eyes. Looking quickly from left to right in a panic, he tried to steady his breathing.

"Are you ok, Roland?!" Thomas asked, alarmed.

"What the hell just happened?" Roland replied in a strained, worried voice.

Thomas jumped over and grabbed the boy by the shoulders. "Roland! What is wrong?"

Roland looked into Thomas' eyes. "I woke in the castle in the middle of my meditation. Everyone was dead, and enemies were attacking the king. I saw Mathias—but he was older—and he was about to kill Father! What just happened? How is this possible?!"

Thomas tried to calm him. "Roland, slow down. It must have been a dream—you were out for quite a while."

Roland knew it was more than a dream. He had heard stories of people with powers called clairtangency. Villagers said such people had "the touch." They had visions in dreams, could feel when someone was sick simply by touching their hands. At this moment, Roland felt the same way. The vision was too vivid—it lingered like a dream that vanishes upon waking.

He finally spoke. "I am ok, Thomas. I must have dozed off and had a nightmare."

Thomas stood, offered his hand, and helped Roland to his feet. "I'm glad to see your color coming back. You were as pale as a ghost. Let's walk back to the castle. I'm sure everything will be fine. Forget the nightmare—you have more important things to deal with."

20

The two friends walked past the stables and around the arena. People were gathering for the upcoming event. Trainers hurried to prepare, running about like ants to their hill. They cleared away anything unneeded, set up a pergola for the royalty, and stretched lengths of chain between the large wooden posts encircling the grounds.

Once they reached the castle, the two entered and saw King Alexander walking toward them.

"AHH, MY BOY, are you ready for the events of the day?"

Roland smiled at his father. "Yes, sir. It's just a sparring match—more like practice, though."

As Roland finished speaking, Queen Scarlett appeared behind the king, Mathias not far behind her. The prince wore chain mail thicker than usual, the rings made of higher-grade steel. Stocky pauldrons sat on his shoulders, each embossed with a striking snake. Gold bordered the edges, with rubies as the snakes' eyes.

On both hips hung a set of twin axes. Their heads were larger than his typical hand axes, with the center cut out. Forged from a strange metal Roland did not recognize, they gleamed brightly. Even in the low castle light, the blades sparkled with razor sharpness. The handles were made of Lignum vitae wood—a rare material Roland only knew from village tales, worth more than most could imagine. The wood never burned, never floated, and never rotted. He

82

didn't know where Mathias had gotten it, though with his wealth, Roland suspected he had simply overpaid.

The handles matched his shoulder guards, worked with gold near the knob and grip. Large iron covers capped the knobs, each set with a red jewel. An overstrike protector—a thick leather collar—wrapped the haft to prevent splitting. Above and below it were engravings Roland had never seen. Above: eight black arrows radiating in a circle, repeated all around. Below: a vertical line with a triangle pointing right, dyed blood red.

Mathias looked fearsome in the outfit.

As Scarlett and Mathias reached them, she smiled. "Good day, son. Are you ready for the tournament today?"

Her breath carried a slight stench of wine, but she was cheerful and outgoing as ever.

Just as Roland began to reply, Mathias butted in. "Are you ready to learn from a master?" he boasted with a devilish grin.

Roland recognized the goading but refused to react. He had played this game before. "Looking forward to it, brother," he said softly, knowing the word would sting.

The queen sensed the tension. "I'm heading out to make sure everything is set up. There will be food and drink for everyone in attendance. Would you like to join me, dear?"

Both Mathias and Alexander answered "Yes" in unison.

"Oh—well, both of you should join me. How about you, Roland?"

The young man smiled politely. "No, thank you, Mother. Thomas and I have a few things to work on before my match. But thank you for the offer."

Mathias bristled again at Roland's use of "Mother."

"Very well," she said, kissing his cheek. "We shall see you in a few hours."

She and the king headed out, Mathias shoulder-checking Roland as he passed.

Thomas laughed under his breath. "See, Roland? Everything is fine."

Roland nodded, though the vision's lingering dread still weighed on him.

"Alright, boy," Thomas said, "let's get you some armor and a shield fitted. The one you've been practicing with has seen better days."

21

The two made their way once more toward the blacksmith.

Horace was happy to see both of them again. "Young master, I have made you a special armor for today's contest. It is a unique chain mail."

Roland smiled and said, "Thank you, Horace, but you did not need to."

Horace shook his head and smiled brightly. "No, no, it was my pleasure. I made the prince one,"—he looked around and whispered—"I was forced to, so I wanted to make you one just as good."

The blacksmith pulled out a blue-gray colored chain mail armor. "It is from a special metal I have been working and experimenting with lately. The blue tint comes from a process I recently learned, and it is very strong. If you put on your gambeson, I can do the final fitting for you."

Roland did as he was asked, and Horace grabbed a few tools and worked on the suit, walking around each side. He hooked and unhooked rings, crimped areas, and moved the mail until it fit Roland just right. Finally, he stood up, took a step back, and admired his work. He set down his tools and spoke in a low, gravelly voice.

"It looks perfect." He cocked his head, staring at his work. "How does it feel, boy?"

Roland flexed, stretched, and bent down with ease before saying, "It is just right. Tight where it should be, and flexible where I need it to be." He picked up his sword and did a few maneuvers to test it even more. "It's great, Horace, thank you so much!"

Horace smiled his toothiest grin. "Oh my, I almost forgot the shield." He rummaged through a pile on one of the tables and pulled one out. "I had the craftsman make it, and then I put my work into it. Gary Robert told me he had some linden wood hidden in the back that he was saving for a special occasion. I traded him a dagger for the wood and his labor."

Horace held it up. It was a pale yellow, about eighteen inches in diameter and three inches thick. Two large rhino heads were carved on either side, stained a gray color. In the center was a large shield boss made of the same material as the chain mail. On the back, two large leather straps with black buckles secured it to Roland's forearm.

Horace handed him the shield, and Roland slipped it on his arm and adjusted the buckle. "It feels good, lightweight, and maneuverable. It's an amazing piece of work—a true piece of art."

Horace put his hands on his wide hips and said, "You look like a real knight now."

Roland was moved that all the people he had relationships and friendships with in the kingdom had treated him so well. Unlike the prince, Roland felt as if they actually liked him instead of fearing him.

"I will put everything in a chest and have it sent to your room," Horace said.

Roland thanked him. He and Thomas left, walking back toward the castle. "I am going to go to my room and relax before the event, try to get my head straight, and make sure I am ready," Roland said with a sigh.

Thomas put his hands on Roland's shoulders and looked him in the eyes. "You are one of, if not the brightest, students I have. You just need to relax and treat it like one of our lessons. He will be more devious and fight dirtier than us, and you cannot fully train for that. Just keep your eyes open and trust in your skill."

Roland put his hands on his mentor's wrists and said, "I will do my very best to make you proud."

Thomas replied, "All I ask for is your best, and you have already made me proud."

They shook each other's forearms and parted ways. Roland went to his room, removed his sword and sheath, and lay in bed, lacing his fingers behind his head. He relaxed and let his thoughts wander as he stared at the ceiling.

22

A few hours later, there was a knock at the door. The trunk from Horace had arrived. He thanked the young man who brought it and dragged it into his room. He opened it up, pulled the gambeson, shield, and chain mail out, and laid them on his bed alongside his sword and sheath.

He put on a clean pair of pants, cleaned his boots, and then put them on. He donned his gambeson and chain mail, then buckled his sword around his waist. Grabbing his shield, he looked at himself in the polished metal disc. He was ready.

The boy walked through the castle toward the arena. On his way, Thomas and all the trainers met him and walked with him. He passed many other people as he went, and he could hear them whispering.

When the entourage reached the arena, Roland saw his parents sitting under the pergola in the shade with Mathias. Both wizards sat on opposite sides of the seating area. He watched the crowd filing in to witness the event—the promise of free food and mead helping to fill the stands.

Gary Robert, the king's squire, bowed to Roland and spoke. "The king has decided to have some events, such as jousting and duels, showing off the other knights' skills, before your event. He has requested that you join him and the queen until then."

87

Roland walked up, bowed to his parents, and sat next to Alexander. He was getting anxious to get this over with. He watched the knights and the trainees show off for the crowd. The jousting had just ended when Roland showed up.

Finally, after the last duels were finished and the crowd's applause died down, Alexander stood and walked to the center of the arena. The crowd went crazy with applause, hoots, and hollers. The noise was deafening. Alexander raised both his hands in the air, and the applause slowly wound down to a hum.

"People of Atheria," he bellowed. "Today is a great day." He paused. "Today, you will see what the future holds for you. What our future rulers have—see the way they will protect you and what they have learned during training. My two sons have both been training for battle and will put on an exhibition for you. They will show you the skills they possess to defend you and our kingdom, if that time ever comes. People of Atheria, my sons, Mathias and Roland!"

The two boys walked out and stood on either side of the king, waving at the crowd. Again, the applause was thunderous, shaking the very ground beneath their feet.

Arthur, the winner of the final match, entered the arena and walked up to the boys. Alexander put his enormous hands on both of their shoulders and said, "Make us proud, boys!"

Arthur stood between them as Alexander exited. "Boys, this is an exhibition. Keep it light but also show your skills—play to the crowd. If one of you gets hurt, go to the corner and yell out that you concede, and I will come in and stop everything. Understand?"

Roland nodded, but Mathias only rolled his eyes.

"Do. You. Understand?" Arthur said more sternly this time.

The prince sneered. "Whatever, let's get this over with. It will be quick, and I have more important things to do."

Arthur looked at Roland, gave him a nod, and went to the chained-off area.

The boys looked each other dead in the eyes. Roland could see the hate burning in his brother's gaze. They took their places and got into their fighting stances.

23

Under the bruised light of an overcast sky, the training yard became a crucible of raw, unbridled intensity. The clash of metal and the unforgiving scrape of leather against dirt formed a grim symphony that underscored every heartbeat.

Roland advanced with measured determination, his eyes betraying a flicker of uncertainty. Mathias, fueled by an all-consuming hatred, was a tempest ready to shatter that resolve. With a guttural snarl echoing from deep within his chest, Mathias exploded forward and upward. His body twisted in mid-air with predatory grace that belied the ferocity in his gaze. His twin axes caught the ambient light, reflecting a cold, steely determination as they sliced through the space between him and Roland.

In that suspended moment, every breath and heartbeat throbbed with the tang of sweat, iron, and impending doom.

Time fractured as Mathias's axes collided with Roland's shoulder armor, a thunderous metallic shriek slicing through the din of battle. With brutal precision, the hooked blades latched on, sending a violent ripple through the air. In a heartbeat, Roland was ripped from his stance and violently flipped over.

The sound of his body colliding with the ground, followed by the clang of his shield striking beside him, was cruel and final—a bone-jarring thud as he skidded to a halt, knee pads scraping wildly against the rough terrain, steel grating against coarse stone.

Mathias landed like a shadow born of darkness itself, a deliberate, predatory presence amidst the chaos. His eyes, cold and merciless, locked onto the disoriented form of Roland. Each step stirred small whirlwinds of dust that mingled with the bitter tang of sweat and blood lingering in the air. His voice cut through the silence like a dagger as he hissed,

"You are nothing but a weakling, destined to crumble beneath my weight."

The bitter air seemed to seep into every crevice, sealing the fate of the moment. Mathias's words carried not only contempt but the promise of further domination—a dark vow that each defeat would knit his disdain tighter. The clash of steel, the echo of ruined ambition, and the weight of venomous hatred were now woven into the very fabric of the training arena.

Roland pushed himself to his feet and said, "Let's try that again."

Mathias rushed him once more. Roland raised his shield. Mathias hooked the top of Roland's shield with the beard of his axe and yanked downward. Roland's head was pulled down with it, and Mathias leapt, driving his knee into Roland's jaw and knocking him backwards. The crowd went wild.

As Roland landed, he rolled backwards and jumped to his feet. He wiped his mouth with the back of his hand. There was blood, but what stung worse was realizing he had fallen for Mathias's cheap shot.

"Do you concede, brother?" the prince asked viciously.

Roland's reply was low and steady. "Not on your life."

"It will be your life!" Mathias screamed as he charged again.

This time, Roland was ready. As the boy closed in, Roland ducked low and slammed his shield into the prince's gut. Lifting with the impact, he tossed Mathias over and behind him. The young prince landed hard on his face, sprawled out across the dirt. Now it was his turn to bleed.

Mathias rose, embarrassed and enraged, the crowd's roar only deepening the humiliation. He crouched low in a barbarian stance, axes in both hands, sneering, blood trailing from the corner of his mouth.

Roland advanced, shield up, sword steady at his side. Mathias lashed out, faster than Roland had expected. Axe against sword, strike against shield, they clashed in a furious rhythm. Roland began to notice a pattern. When the moment came, he slipped around the boy's guard and smacked him hard on the backside, sending Mathias jumping.

The young prince grew even angrier. "How dare you!" he screamed.

They met again, slash for slash, Mathias driving Roland back. Roland realized his own attacks were falling into a rhythm the prince would soon exploit. So, when Mathias swung both axes down, Roland dropped low, swept the prince's feet from under him, and leapt over, returning to his stance. Mathias went down hard.

He rose again, dropping to one knee. Roland recognized the move—the last time Mathias had thrown dirt into an opponent's eyes. But to his surprise, the trick never came. The crowd quieted. Roland lowered his guard slightly as he approached.

"Do you con—"

Before he could finish, Mathias lunged upward, slashing at Roland's face. Roland leaned back, but both axes still raked the edges of his cheeks, slicing beneath his eyes and leaving twin trails of blood.

"NEVER!" Mathias roared, swinging wildly. Roland managed to raise his shield just in time. He tightened his grip on his sword, and as soon as an opening appeared, he rammed the hilt into Mathias's gut. The prince dropped his axes, stumbling back. Roland followed with a Spartan kick to his chest, sending him sprawling once more.

The crowd erupted again as Roland spun back around, his sword back into a ready stance.

Mathias, gasping, rolled onto his hands and knees. Hurt, but unwilling to yield, he reached for the lengths of chain draped on the wooden pillars surrounding the arena. Roland didn't see until it was too late—Mathias swung a chain like a whip, wrapping it around Roland's sword and yanking it from his grasp.

Now defenseless, Roland faced Mathias as he seized another chain and swung it down repeatedly, whip and pull, whip and pull, each strike edging closer. Roland rolled away until he caught the chain, letting it coil painfully around his arm. With a brutal tug, he dragged the prince towards him and hurled the chain aside.

The boys exchanged blow after blow, the crowd in a frenzy. Both landed a punch at the same time, fists slamming into each other's jaws with such force that they collapsed together. Exhausted and battered, each crawled for their weapons. Roland reached his shield first.

Mathias seized an axe and hurled it with such force that it sank deep into Roland's shield, the tip bursting through the back. Roland wrenched it free as he regained his footing.

At that moment, Arthur had seen enough. He rushed between them, shouting, "It's a draw!"

But that was not good enough for Mathias. Shoving Arthur aside, he pressed forward, axe swinging as Roland defended with the other one.

Arthur tried again, grappling with Mathias, but the prince elbowed him in the gut and raised his axe to strike the defenseless trainer. The other instructors ran forward, knowing Mathias was lost to his rage.

Before he could strike, both boys froze in place—paralyzed. Roland felt the grip too, stiff and unyielding. The king had commanded the court wizards to end the spectacle before it descended further into disgrace. Like puppeteers, they maneuvered the brothers, forcing them to drop their weapons and face the crowd.

Roland let it happen. Mathias thrashed against the invisible bonds to no avail.

Then Alexander strode between them, seizing their hands and raising them high. His voice boomed across the yard:

"It is a draw!!"

He fixed Mathias with a sharp look that silenced his struggle. Once the wizards saw it, they released their grip.

The crowd erupted in thunderous applause, cheering for both boys.

Thomas came to Roland's side and escorted him from the arena, while Mathias stalked away alone, a scowl darkening his face. Megendra was waiting for him beyond the chains.

The crowd roared once more at their exit, then gradually dispersed, sated with blood, spectacle, food, and mead for the day.

24

Roland's face was covered in his own blood, and his cuts were very deep. Thomas grabbed a small jar from his belt. It was a mixture of honey and lemon. He applied it to the boy's face after wiping it clean with a wet rag. Roland winced from the sting of the lemon burning in the cut.

"This will definitely leave a scar," Thomas said. "You handled yourself very well. I would have probably lost my temper and ended up hurting the prince worse than you did."

Roland's body was exhausted, and he sat on the nearest log to rest.

"I wholly did not expect him to grab the chain. I guess I have more training to do to learn to expect the worst and improvise on the fly," the boy said through the pain. "I also think he realizes I am not a pushover. I hope he now knows he can only beat me by cheating."

Thomas looked at Roland. "In war, there are no rules and no cheating. That is all he has on you." He grabbed a small piece of cloth and stuck it to the honey on Roland's wounds. "He looks like he is just as battered and bruised as you are. He doesn't have any deep facial cuts, but his face is starting to swell and bruise. And that move where you threw him definitely left a mark."

Roland stood up as he saw the king approaching. Everyone surrounding Roland bowed as the king reached them.

"That was a fine show, my boy. A little more aggressive than I had first thought, and I was led to believe it would be. You have unequivocally come far from the first time we met. I am surprised you have learned so much in so little time. Are you okay? You look a bit… rough?"

Roland grimaced again and said, "I am good, Father, just a bit tired. Thank you for your praise—it means the world to me."

Alexander smiled and said, "You have made me proud, son. I know that in the future I will be able to count on you to protect the kingdom and its people."

Roland lowered his head so the king would not see him blush or see the tears forming in his eyes. This made him feel worthy.

25

At the other end of the arena, Megendra and Mathias were walking back towards the castle.

"You had a chance, and you failed!" Megendra sneered under his hood.

"He was better than I expected!" the prince quipped back.

"You underestimated him. You did not do your job and assess your opponent. You had plenty of time to watch him train," Megendra said with a vicious tone.

Mathias was pissed. "Then why did you not step in? You could have taken him out in an instant."

The sorcerer gave him a look that made the young man recoil slightly. "How did you expect me to do that? If I did anything in front of your parents or Seoul, I would be at the gallows right now, waiting for my head to be removed from my body. The boy will only get better as he ages. He will be a problem. We need to figure out another way for you to take the throne."

Mathias said, "I am not scared of him. He is nothing more than a peasant to me."

Megendra took a second to respond. "We will deal with him when the time comes. For now, you need to heal from your embarrassing loss and make everyone believe that your actions were with good intent—that you were not trying to murder or maim him."

The pair arrived back at the castle. Mathias stomped back towards his chamber as Megendra disappeared down one of the corridors. As the prince passed by Ami, he grabbed her hard by the arm.

"Ow, you are hurting me!"

He squeezed harder. "Shut your mouth, wench! Summon one of the nursemaids to my room." He pushed her away as he let her loose.

Ami grabbed her arm where the prince had hurt her and did as she was bidden. The nurse came a few minutes later and tended to Mathias.

26

Roland excused himself from Thomas and Arthur and headed to the castle. Seoul joined him on his walk.

"Your skill shone out there. You did well today."

Roland thanked him. "I think I am going to get some rest, but I would like to talk to you later. I had a… dream… during a meditation session."

"Was it a dream or a vision?" the mage asked.

Roland looked at him, knowing full well he knew more than he was letting on. "I am not really sure—that is what I want to talk to you about, later."

The mage looked at him probingly as they reached the castle. "Come see me once you have healed."

He handed Roland a small vial from inside the arm of his robe. It was filled with a greenish-yellow liquid that squirmed around inside, as if it were alive. It glowed in the dim light of the castle.

"Take this after you eat—it will help the healing process."

Roland stuffed it in his pouch and said, "Thank you, I will."

Roland headed towards his room, and just like Megendra, Seoul seemed to disappear.

Roland passed by the kitchen and spotted Ami. She ran to him and wrapped her arms around him. Roland noticed the bruise starting to form on Ami's arm and asked, "What happened to your arm?"

She slunk down and said softly, "Mathias."

Roland was visibly angry, but he knew he was in no shape to go after him. "If he touches you again, let me know, and I will take care of it."

Ami perked up a bit. "Ok, I will—I promise," she said meekly.

"You looked good out there. How are your wounds? You must be hungry." She touched the cloth stuck to his face.

Roland smiled as she touched him, and at how quickly she perked up. "I am hungry, and I will make a full recovery."

Ami started to run off and hollered back, "Hold on, I will be right back." She disappeared into the kitchen.

She came back just as fast as she left, with a bowl of dried beef, a roll, a pear, and some nuts. He took the bowl from her and cupped her cheek with his hand, rubbing her face with his thumb.

"Thank you, this is great."

She blushed at his touch and ran back towards the kitchen. She turned and looked at him, cheeks flushed.

"Bye, Roland."

She vanished back into the kitchen.

Roland went to his room and removed his gear slowly, placing it in the trunk as he did. He unbuckled his sword and scabbard and laid them on top of the trunk. The boy sat down, ate his food, and drank the vial Seoul had given him.

27

The thoughts of the battle ran through his head as he passed out. He slept hard and deep; no dreams came to him that night.

When Roland woke up, it was well past sundown. He felt better—not fully one hundred percent, but better. He peeled the cloth Thomas had applied to his face off and ran his fingers across the cuts. He was surprised to find they had already scabbed over. He was still sore when he stood, but not nearly as sore as he had been when he laid down earlier. It was time, he decided, to go talk to Seoul.

When he opened his door, he saw a tray of food laid out with a note from Ami. The note had a heart drawn on it. He brought it inside and ate quickly, not realizing until then how hungry he was. On his way to see the mage, he dropped off the tray in the kitchen. He was surprised by how quiet the castle was at this time of night—it was peaceful, almost serene, and quite beautiful.

He reached the dark staircase, and as he descended, candles flared to life, lighting his way. Slowly, he made his way down to the sanctum. The large door stood open, as if Seoul already knew he was coming—and most likely, he did.

"Ahh, Roland, you are awake. I thought my potion would keep you asleep much longer. How do you feel?" the mage asked, his back still turned.

Roland sat near the fire in the middle of the room. "I feel better than I thought would be possible. Thank you for your elixir." He cracked his neck, then asked, "Can we talk about my dream… or vision… or whatever it was?"

The old man turned slowly toward him, speaking with deliberate calm. "Tell me about it. I want every detail you can remember."

Roland sighed and took a deep breath. "Thomas was teaching me to meditate, and once I relaxed, I woke up—but I was in the castle in what felt like the future. I saw most of the castle guards murdered, and a man who looked like the prince, but older, was about to murder the king. Then I woke up."

The wizard stroked his beard as he thought. "It sounds more like a vision—or foresight—than a dream. Your birth mother had them also."

Roland perked up. "You knew my mother?"

Seoul smiled. "Yes, I knew both her and Scarlett from a very young age. Your grandmother brought her here to see me when she was about your age. She was having visions, too. She thought she was sick, that something was wrong with her. I told her she had a power, and there was no way to make them stop. When she asked me what she could do, I told her to be aware of her visions, but to keep them to herself so as not to be mocked, or thought a witch, or worse. The visions she told me of did come true—most of them, anyway. After that, I only saw her in passing. It seems she passed that gift on to you."

Roland was silent for a moment, then asked, "Are you going to give me the same advice you gave her? Do you think my vision will come to pass?"

Again, Seoul took his time to answer, stroking his beard. "Since you are living here, in my presence, and since it involves the king, I would like you to consult with me whenever you have one of these visions. Be aware of what you see, but also keep it between us. No need to cause a panic—or give Mathias a reason to call you deranged and have you thrown into the dungeon, or exiled."

Hierax cawed at Roland. The boy walked over to the bird, stroking his head and chest as he mulled over what had been said. "I can do that. I've had similar dreams before, but most fade away when I wake. I'll keep a journal by my bed and write down anything I remember."

As he turned toward the door, Seoul said, "We will get through this. I would like to start working with Hierax in the near future. He could be a good ally to you."

Roland raised an eyebrow. "I would like that. I'm going to get some more rest, so I'm ready to start training again tomorrow. Thank you for everything."

Seoul bowed to him as he left. Roland walked back to his room, his mind crowded with thoughts. Once he lay down, he tossed and turned before finally falling asleep.

28

Over the next few years, things in the castle changed.

Dinners with the family were mostly calm. Mathias would not look at or speak to Roland unless absolutely necessary—if he even bothered to show his face. Meanwhile, Ami and Roland grew closer, their young love quietly blossoming. At night, he would sneak out to meet her in the fields, where they would lie under the stars and talk—among other things.

Roland also grew closer to his father, often attending meetings with his advisors. He sat in the war room with the knights while plans for defending the castle and village from rebellion or attack were discussed. He developed a taste for mead, drinking with his father and having serious conversations about running the kingdom—both in the present and in the future. He accompanied him on hunts, and they often brought most of the kills back to the villagers. Roland would also go into the village to speak with the people directly, listening to their grievances and learning what help they needed.

Most of the people loved both Roland and the king. But there were others who despised them. Some believed the king had not done enough during the plague. Others hated

Roland out of jealousy—that a "street rat" who was once like them had risen to royalty.

Roland's training with Thomas also continued. He started training with Hierax also. After Roland's fight with Mathias, Thomas adjusted the regimen. The king and queen would sometimes come down to watch, just as they had once done for Mathias before he quit. But whenever Mathias saw them watching Roland, his hatred grew, and he began to resent his father more and more.

He wanted to murder Roland in his sleep, but at Megendra's urging, he held back. Instead, he began surrounding himself with people who hated both his father and Roland. Many were scoundrels who hurt people for sport—those were the ones he recruited most eagerly.

Bandits and gangs operated in the countryside, just outside the village, attacking and robbing travelers. They had even robbed a few royal carriages, blaming the attacks on the natives living on the far side of the island. Their luck ended, however, when they tried to rob a carriage guarded by royal soldiers. Quite a few of the bandits were killed in the clever trap devised by Roland and the king. After that, the bandits turned to preying on their own countrymen and weary travelers.

Many of Mathias's companions came from these gangs. Some were failed or expelled guard trainees, rejected for lack of discipline, character, morals, or talent. They were the ones Mathias surrounded himself with the most. In the streets of the castle's bustling metropolis, he was often seen with them at his side, almost like a ragtag personal guard. If

anyone came too close, they would assault them—
sometimes brutally. They were notorious, and most people
learned to steer clear.

Mathias dined with his family less and less over the next
four years. On the rare occasions that he did, he spoke little,
never laughed, never asked about the state of the kingdom,
and offered nothing of value in any conversation he did
speak to.

29

Roland never really knew when his birthday was, so in
the castle, they always celebrated on the anniversary of him
coming to live with them. On his twentieth birthday,
Alexander demanded that Mathias be at dinner that night
with the family.

"Roland shows up for your birthday dinner, so you
should show up for his. Plus, I have news that will affect
both of you boys and the kingdom as a whole," Alexander
said.

The prince was not happy about it. "Fine, I will be there,"
he answered. He stared his father in the eyes for a second,
nodded, and then walked away to meet his entourage for the
day.

Later that night, Roland, Alexander, and Scarlett were
sitting at the table, starting in on dinner. Mathias walked in
about fifteen minutes later, after the food had already been
served.

"Where have you been? I told you earlier to be here!" the
king shouted.

104

Mathias quipped back, "Am I not here? You told me to be here for dinner, and I am here."

The king, looking older now with less hair—what remained white and grey—turned bright red. Scarlett, also looking older, put her hand on Alexander's knee and gave him a look, silently telling him to let it go and stay seated. Mathias had a smirk on his face as he greedily shoveled food onto his plate.

"What is this news you prattled on about earlier?" the prince asked.

The king's face grew red again. "I would advise you to watch your tone. I am still your king. And your father," he said in a low, brooding voice.

Mathias waved his turkey leg around in a go on type manner.

Alexander took a big swig of his mead and then said, "We are not getting any younger—"

Mathias interrupted. "No kidding!"

The king's face was growing past red and nearly purple with anger, but then a smirk spread across his lips as he stood.

"I have decided that when I step down, or when I meet my Lord, I am appointing Roland as my heir."

Roland choked on his food, as did Mathias before spitting it out.

"What are you talking about? I am your only TRUE heir! He is no better than a farmhand at best!" the young prince screamed.

"What did you expect, boy? He has been by my side in the war room and with me when I have met with my advisors. They all respect and trust him—as do the people of our kingdom. He goes out to the villages and talks to the people about their concerns and needs. You, on the other hand, surround yourself with thieves and bandits. You push everyone around, and they are scared of you. You have given me no choice!" The king screamed back at his son, food and spittle flying from his mouth.

"Then what will be my position? Prince until he dies? I can't believe this bastard is getting my rightful spot—my birthright," Mathias said, pointing at Roland.

"I need you to be a commander of the knights. But you also need to get back to training before that can even happen. How can you lead if you haven't put in the time the others have?" the king said.

Mathias was furious. "I'm supposed to be sent to die for you? I was born to order from the throne, not the battlefield!"

"Roland," the king declared, "would you be willing to fight for me, lead my knights into battle, and run the kingdom?"

Roland looked him in the eye. "No."

The king was speechless. He just stared.

"I'm willing to fight for OUR kingdom, in Your name. The kingdom is my priority. I will serve it and protect it in any way that I am asked to do."

Alexander walked over next to Roland and looked him in the face. "Then what I'm asking you to do is lead the kingdom when I step away from the throne. Protect it as I have done. Will you accept this? Will you be the next in line to take the throne?"

At this, Mathias threw his plate across the room, smashed his chair against the wall, and stormed out. Everyone from the kitchen had started watching the commotion since Mathias first began screaming.

Once he was gone, the kitchen staff returned to their work. Scarlett drank the rest of her goblet of wine and poured another—something she had been doing a lot of in the last year. The three of them sat silently, finishing their dinner.

Once Roland had finished, he excused himself and kissed his mother on the forehead before heading out. All of the last hour's commotion seemed so familiar, but he wasn't sure how. As he passed the kitchen, he gave Ami a wink. As always, her cheeks turned a bright red.

30

Roland decided to head up to the top of the tower to gather his thoughts while looking over the kingdom and the beautiful star-filled night. He saw Mathias near the entrance of the castle. He and his entourage were headed in, and as usual, they were armed. But Roland noticed they were armed more than usual, and Mathias was screaming.

It all came back at once. The reason all this seemed familiar was that it had been in his visions. Roland rushed down to his room to grab his sword.

Once he reached his room, he heard the chaos outside the castle and knew what was about to happen. He ran through the halls toward the chamber he knew the king would be in. When he arrived, he was relieved to see that his father was still seated on the throne—the traitors hadn't made it in yet. He quickly pulled five of the guardsmen in with him.

"Get in here and protect your king!" he yelled.

Alexander asked, "What is going on?"

Roland replied, "I think Mathias means to kill your father."

The king looked shocked. "No, I know he was upset, but not enough to try this!"

Roland met his eyes. "He is the one leading the attack. I don't see any other reason he would kill your royal guard unless he was after you."

As soon as he finished, the door was kicked open and four of the Mathias's men rushed in. A spear flew through the doorway, killing one guard instantly, and the others pressed the attack. Roland joined the fight, helping the remaining guards cut down the marauders.

Then Mathias strode in, hurling an axe that struck a guard square in the head, killing him . He walked up and yanked his weapon free with a crunching sound as it tore from the lifeless skull. The other three guards tried to engage him but were swiftly dispatched.

Mathias rushed the Roland. He swung both axes, fending off the swords of two guards. As a third charged, Mathias hooked the man's sword and drug it down, driving it into the path of the oncoming soldier. The man was impaled, and Mathias followed with a slash across another guard's throat.

"Back away," he ordered the last guardsman.

The man rushed out to call for help as more attackers came.

"Mathias, what are you doing? I am your king, and I order you to back down!" the king shouted.

"Shut up, old man. I'll deal with you when I'm done with this swine!" Mathias scoffed back. His eyes locked onto Roland. "Here you are, licking his boots. Plotting against me. I knew I should have killed you the first night!"

Roland gave a small laugh. "You tried, remember? I bested you then, and I will best you now. Back away and leave, or I will not hesitate to take your life."

"You can try, *brother*, but nothing will stop me this time. I'll reopen and deepen those scars on your face. No one stands between us now."

Roland readied his stance. "Your arrogance will be your downfall. If you think you can get past me, then test me. I assure you, the king will be alive this time tomorrow."

Mathias hurled an axe at Roland, but Roland deflected it. Mathias caught the deflected weapon midair as he charged, sliding on his knees to slice Roland's legs out from beneath him. Roland leapt over him and spun back into position. This time, Roland charged, sword swinging. The clash of weapons rang through the hall.

Roland cut Mathias across the ribs, splitting his shirt and opening up a new wound. Blood poured freely, and the prince snarled. Mathias countered with a slice across Roland's shoulder, cutting down his bicep. Both men bled, neither willing to yield.

Roland swung down hard, but Mathias caught the blow on his crossed axes. He kicked Roland square in the chest, sending him to the floor. Roland's sword slid just out of reach.

Mathias raised his weapons for the killing strike—when a piercing cry filled the chamber. Heirax flew through the doorway like a bullet, talons striking Mathias' left eye and nearly tearing it out. The hawk ripped and shredded the flesh around his face, tearing into him as if he were prey. Its beak drove deep into his head, drawing blood and pulling clumps of hair.

Mathias howled with pain but managed to grab the bird and hurl it to the ground. With one brutal stomp, he snapped its neck. Heirax's body twitched and jerked before falling still.

The distraction gave Roland time to roll away and rise, though his sword was still beyond reach. Mathias seized an axe embedded in the floor and charged. He hurled it at Roland—but Roland caught it and instantly threw it back. The blade struck Mathias's armed hand, severing two fingers before burying itself in the handle of his other axe. Both weapons clattered to the ground as Mathias dropped to his knees in agony.

Roland rushed forward, reclaimed his sword, and kicked the axes aside. He pressed the blade to his brother's throat.

"For the crime of attempted regicide, I find you guilty. The punishment is death." Roland raised his sword for the final blow.

"NO! Don't kill him!" Scarlett's scream rang out as she entered. Arthur and Thomas close behind with weapons drawn.

Roland hesitated.

"Please, Roland. Anything but death."

Roland knelt before his mother. "He tried to kill Father—and for all I know, you would be next. He deserves death!"

The king rose from his throne and stepped beside his wife. "He may deserve death, Roland—along with all those who followed him. But killing our son, your brother, is wrong. Thomas, bring the shackles. Gather the traitors and chain them."

Roland's grip faltered. "Will he spend his life in the dungeon?"

"I'd rather die," Mathias spat.

Alexander's voice was steady. "You won't die today, nor in the dungeon. You and your followers will be banished. You will be sent far beyond my kingdom, to the lands of the natives on the south side of the island. If you dare return, you will be put to death."

As the years passed on the King ruled until he became sick, eventually dying in his sleep. The queen had begun to drink more and more after Mathias' exile, barely ever leaving her room. A few months later, the alcohol finally took its toll on Scarlett. The queen died of alcohol poisoning in her room all alone, heartbroken by her family.

Now that he was the heir, Roland ascended to the throne. Taking his rightful place as king.

PART TWO
THE AFTERMATH

1

Many years after King Alexander exiled his son Mathias to the land of the natives at the southernmost part of the island, we see the kingdom of Atheria flourishing. Roland's men had been patrolling the border the entire time, keeping an eye on the comings and goings of the people of the now-named kingdom of Zion. Megendra suggested the name, saying it meant "Kingdom of Heaven," and after all, Mathias thought he was a god among men. Mathias also kept men patrolling the border. A few times, he had tried sending his men to spy on the kingdom, but Roland's knights stopped them before they had gotten very far. Megendra and Seoul were able to see into each other's kingdoms for a short period of time before they started blocking each other's magic. Mathias and Roland always called the men on the opposite border spies, and in reality, they were.

One night, no different than any other, as the men at the border were on patrol, they noticed a bright twinkle in the sky. It looked to be a shooting star, but they realized it was getting larger by the minute and changing. The diamond-like twinkle turned into a large orange ball with a tail of what looked like dragon fire burning behind it. The fireball grew bigger and bigger as it came closer to the Earth. The men could feel the heat emanating from it. They watched as it hit the earth with a deafening sound. When it struck, the ground shook and trembled ferociously, shaking the entire island and knocking the men from their horses. It plowed into the ground, digging deeper as the trench grew longer. A plume of smoke so large it could be seen for miles shot into the sky. The flames that trailed from it scorched everything in its path, destroying all within fifty yards on each side. The embers floated like red fireflies in the dark. The deep black from the scorched trees and plants shone bright like obsidian against the night sky. Once the men were able to calm their horses, they headed toward the rock in the ground. When they laid eyes on it, they decided to ride as fast as possible back to their respective kings.

Ash, the son of Thomas and Eve, was the first one back to the castle. He woke his father first and told him what he had seen. Thomas then had the king woken up. Thomas and Ash gathered a few of the best troops and pulled the rest of the border guards into the war room while they waited for their king.

On the southernmost part of the island, the spies were also returning to their castle and had the king's esquire wake him. They gathered a few of the king's men and told them to be ready to depart soon.

Roland sauntered into the war room, rubbing his eyes and yawning loudly. "Why have I been woken up? I hope it's important."

Ash stood up. "Lord, there has been an event at the border. A star from the sky has crashed there. I'm not sure if it's important or not, but Mathias' men looked at it and rode off toward their castle. It may be worth something, and we didn't want Mathias to have it all to himself," the boy said quickly.

Seoul walked in unnoticed, as he usually did. "My lord, I can feel the star's power radiating in the air. I suggest you go to it and have it brought back for me to examine," the sorcerer said in a low voice, startling everyone in the room.

"What type of power is it?" the king asked.

"The magical type," Seoul said.

"Gather my men. Make sure to get a flatbed carriage with a block-and-tackle pulley so we can hoist and transport the star."

Ash said, "It's ready and waiting."

Roland was proud of the boy Thomas had raised. "Good job. I'll meet you down at the stables soon," the king said.

Roland was awake now and sprinted to his room, grabbed his sword, and dressed. He kissed Ami and his daughter Megan as he headed out. A few minutes later, he arrived at the stables, and they all headed off.

2

Mathias was annoyed that he was roused awake. "What the hell is so important that you woke me? If this isn't important, someone is being beheaded," the king said angrily.

Brody, the king's top border knight and spy, told Mathias, "A star from the sky has fallen on the border."

"Why the hell would I care about that?"

Megendra spoke up. "The star has some sort of power. Roland and his men are headed toward it. We need to take possession of it. Gather your men and go retrieve it."

Hearing that Roland wanted it made Mathias want it more. "Suit up, men! We're going to make sure Roland doesn't get it—it is ours." Mathias grabbed his dual axes, put on his clothes, and headed out, following Brody to the crash site.

3

Both parties arrived within minutes of each other. Mathias' men were holding off Roland's men, and vice versa. Roland spotted Mathias, who was sauntering in on his horse.

"Be gone, brother. This land is mine, and so is the star that crashed on it."

Mathias quipped back, "None of this land is rightfully yours. You stole it from me. It was my birthright. So it is you who will be leaving—dead or alive, the choice is yours."

While the two men were bickering back and forth, no one noticed that the rock in the crater was starting to pulse with lights, growing brighter as time went on.

"It will be you who will die. I let you live long ago after you betrayed our family. I have left you alone to rule what you call a 'kingdom,' but if you cross me, I won't hesitate to end you here and now," Roland said sternly.

"I should have killed you in that arena when we were children. Letting you live was a mistake I will never make again!" Mathias screamed at him.

At this point, the horses started to spook, rearing up and acting agitated. They could sense the incoming danger. Roland and Mathias looked around, and by the time they saw the object, it was too late. The light from the comet flooded the sky and exploded. The horses and men closest to the crater were instantly vaporized. The explosion caused an air-blast, knocking most of the men—including the kings—from their horses. The meteor threw two small pieces opposite ways, while the rest of the star was incinerated into ash that blew away with the wind. Mathias' men who survived remounted any living horses and retreated, leaving their king behind.

Mathias picked himself up after being thrown against a tree, breaking his arm. He spotted the piece of the star closest to him, grabbed it with his cloak, and threw it in the bag on his horse. He took off toward his kingdom as quickly as he could.

Roland's men were a little luckier than their opposition. Most were far enough back that they were just knocked off their horses, though a few had died from their injuries, and a few more were badly wounded from the explosion. Roland himself was lucky enough to be thrown into a pile of brush that had been made by a fox or possibly a coyote.

"Are you okay, Roland?" Thomas asked after running over to his king.

"I'm fine, Thomas, thank you. Please gather our dead and bring them back. I need to see if any of the rock is left."

Thomas helped him up. "Ash found a piece. He wrapped it in a piece of his cloak. I'll have him put it in your saddlebag."

The remaining men gathered their dead, laid them on the flatbed carriage, and headed home. Once they pulled into the underground stables, the survivors went back to their rooms, and the wounded went to see the nurses who had been called in earlier. Roland decided to stay down there with his dead. He unsaddled his horse and put him back in his stable. Then he pulled the cloak containing the fallen star out of his saddlebag.

4

The piece was the size of an inflated pig-bladder ball, and very lightweight. It had a chameleon-like color to it, shifting from black to blue to red to green as Roland turned it. He pulled the rock from the cloth and held it in his hand.

"How is this rock worth the lives of so many of my men?" Roland said as he walked toward the cart with his fallen soldiers. He looked at them. "I'm so sorry I caused this. You deserved better," he said solemnly.

As he stood there with his head down, the rock flew from his hand and started floating above the dead soldiers. It began to spin above the cart, its colors pulsing brilliantly. A beam of blue light shot down on the men as Roland stood there bewildered and confused. The light circled the men, lifting the bodies as it encased them in its glow. It coursed in and out of their chests and arms like a worm burrowing through dirt. Then, just as suddenly as it had begun, it set them down gently, went dark, and fell to the cart with a loud thud.

Roland grabbed the cloth, wrapped the now lifeless rock, and put it back in his saddlebag. As he turned back toward the cart holding the men, he noticed them moving. The men sat up, looking as confused as the king himself. One of them noticed Roland, jumped to his feet, and stood at attention. The other two men noticed and did the same.

"Sire," the first one said in an official voice.

Roland walked over and circled around the men. When he came back to stand in front of them, he asked, "Are you men okay? Are you injured?"

The men looked confused. One spoke up: "Majesty, last I remember, we were with you at the site of the fallen rock. After that, it's a blur. Then I woke up here, with you."

The other two shook their heads in agreement and mumbled "yes" under their breath. The king touched their faces as he walked back and forth from man to man.

"Sire, what has happened?" one asked.

Roland took a few steps back. "I'm not sure. But God must not be ready for you yet. Go have Seoul look you over, then you can return to your families."

The men looked at each other for a moment, then walked out.

Roland sat on the edge of the cart and tried to comprehend what had just happened. He decided to brush and feed his horse before he went to consult Seoul. Maybe he would have some answers.

5

Mathias also had an interaction with his piece of the stone. He arrived back at his stables, holding his broken arm in pain. He unmounted his horse, grabbed the rock from the saddlebag, and threw the reins at the stable boy. In the back of the stable, there was a waiting area where Mathias would often wait while his horse was being tacked up. He headed back there to be alone and sulk over his men abandoning him. Heads would roll for that kind of cowardice, he thought.

He sat on a daybed in the back corner and lit a lantern. Looking at his arm in disgust, he could see it was definitely broken—the bone was about to push through his skin. He knew he would have to see either Megendra or a healer soon, but he wanted to calm down first. He unwrapped the rock and rolled it in his good hand. Anger burned in him—not only had he broken his arm, but Roland seemed to have beaten him again, and for what? This stone?

As his anger grew, the stone began to vibrate in his hand. Mathias dropped it next to him on the daybed. The stone levitated above his arm, still vibrating. It twisted and turned in the air, shooting bright purple, blue, and black light from every jagged edge. Then, in an instant—so fast Mathias almost missed it—the stone spat a black fluid onto his broken arm. As soon as it hit his skin, the stone dropped, and the gooey, fleshy substance spread out like a spider, legs stretching in every direction to encase his arm. The pain was immediate and searing.

Mathias screamed from the excruciating agony running through his arm. Once the black goo fully enveloped it, it began to squeeze. He could see his arm shifting beneath the surface, feeling the broken bone move, causing even more pain. He fell from the bed, writhing on the floor in pure torment. Finally, the pain subsided. The goo sank into his arm, leaving behind a blackened, metallic-looking texture.

Mathias ran his hand over it. If he hadn't known better, he would have sworn it was metal—except it was still flexible, pliable. He tapped it with a riding crop: no pain, though he could still feel the pressure, like a numb sensation. He looked around and found a pitchfork. He tapped his arm with the handle: no pain. He struck harder: still nothing. He slammed it across his arm until the handle shattered, and still felt no pain. Then he took the sharp, forked end and stabbed at his arm, bracing for discomfort. But as the metal prongs struck, they bent against his arm.

He tossed the fork aside and stared in amazement. Not even a scratch or scrape. He went over to a pillar near the entrance and slammed his arm into it—the wood shattered, sending splinters everywhere. Mathias grinned. He had an idea. He wrapped the rock back up and headed straight for Megendra, determined to find a way to weaponize this magic stone.

6

About an hour later, Roland went to see Seoul. The sorcerer was bent over a cauldron, writing something on a parchment beside him. He looked up at the king as he finished.

"Good morning, my king. I assume you are here to inquire about your men?" Seoul already knew what had happened—he had seen it, and felt it, in his mind as it occurred, and spoken to the men who were brought back to life.

"As always, you are correct, my friend," the king said tiredly. "What do you think? Are they possessed, living dead—or were they never dead in the first place?"

Seoul answered in his usual monotone voice. "If I didn't know what had happened, I would say they were never injured at all. They are in perfect shape. Better than before, from my findings. From what I have read in my grimoire, the stone may be like the talisman of life that has been written about. But other than that, I have found nothing on it.

"What I did see, and was writing, was about Megendra and Mathias. They don't see the power it has the way we do. I think the stone enhances the morals and characteristics of its owner. Megendra thinks it can be best used as a weapon. I wasn't able to see much more before he realized I was spying through the crow's eye."

Roland stroked his beard, perplexed. "What are your thoughts?"

Seoul asked to see Roland's current sword. "You've had this blade a long time. It is battle-worn, but I think we can do the same as Mathias. We can melt the rock down along with your current blade and have our blacksmith forge a new weapon using the same techniques he used to create this one."

Roland considered. "Can we treat the rock like any other metal? Is it even able to be melted down—and what kind of reaction will putting it to the flame cause?"

"I will work with the blacksmith and protect him if need be," Seoul replied.

"Okay, Seoul. We can talk to Horace and his son about crafting you a new sword. But first I need some sleep—it's been a long night." Roland left Seoul's sanctum and headed to bed, his mind heavy with new questions.

7

Meanwhile, Mathias and Megendra headed to the blacksmith's shop. Mathias had already sent one of his servants to wake the blacksmith, Nort, and ensure he would be there once they arrived.

As the pair arrived, Nort had just gotten the lanterns lit and the fires restoked in the forges.

"Welcome, m'lord, what can I do for you on this early morning?"

Megendra spoke up. "You will take this ingot of the meteorite we have and forge it into a weapon."

It was Nort's turn to speak. "May I see it?"

Mathias pulled the rock from his pocket and let it shake loose from the cloth onto the table between them. Nort's hand reached toward the dead-looking rock on the table.

"Do not touch it with your hands," Megendra spoke firmly. "Pick it up with your clamps."

Nort walked over to his wall of tools and grabbed a set of tongs. He picked up the rock carefully and examined it closely. Taking a small cross-peen hammer, he tapped lightly on it. When it didn't scratch, he struck it harder, and still no damage appeared. Nort set it down and steadied himself.

"This rock is very hard," he admitted. "I'm not sure if my forge fires can get hot enough. Also, with such a small piece, I can't make anything very large."

The pair looked at each other, then back at Nort. Mathias said, "Megendra will work his magic to stoke the flames. He will match the heat that hell itself produces, if needed. I need a set of forged battle axes. Use ironwood and leather for the handles, and use some of the tungsten that was mined to add to the rock. Do not fail me, or I will have my sorcerer torture you slowly, causing you pain you cannot imagine with his magic. Do you understand?"

Nort nodded, lowering his eyes. "Yes, sir. I will get to work right away."

Megendra and Mathias walked to the entrance together as Nort began his preparations behind them.

"I will stay here and help this simpleton make your weapons," Megendra told Mathias. "You need to get some sleep and be ready for the oncoming battle."

Mathias nodded and headed back to his room, while Megendra and Nort got to work. They labored through the night, stoking the flames to rival those of dragon's fire and hellfire. By early the next afternoon, the forging was done. The blacksmith dipped the twin heads into the oil for the last time to harden them. He then began working on the inlay and the handles while Megendra returned to his sanctum.

8

Roland and Seoul woke early the next morning and headed down to Horace's shop. Once there, they explained to Horace and his son what they were looking to do. They warned them of the possible dangers and of what they hoped to accomplish, assuring them that Seoul would be there the whole time to protect and assist.

"There will be a great reward for you if you can do as I've asked," Roland said, placing a hand on the blacksmith's shoulder.

"It would be my honor, my king," Horace replied. "I forged your first sword and hope to surpass its quality this time."

Roland smiled. "You are an artist at your craft, and I look forward to seeing what you can do."

Horace went over to his son, who had already begun adding fuel to the fire.

"Seoul." Roland said, "Be cautious and protect our friend. Come get me when it is finished, please."

"I will, my king," Seoul answered. The two clasped wrists in a firm shake and parted ways.

All day, Horace and the sorcerer worked. Between the blacksmith's experience and the wizard's magic, they were able to melt the rock into a glowing molten metal. It wasn't like anything Horace had ever dealt with. Most molten metal glowed a bright orange or red; this glowed a brilliant turquoise blue, like the ocean.

Once they poured it into a mold, it hardened almost immediately. Again, the two men combined their skills to heat the new metal into a workable state. Horace pounded the metal into a shape he liked, then he melted down and added it to the mold into the blue heat of the rock. Over and over, they heated, folded, and forged the glowing metal into the shape they needed.

Finally, it took its final form. The blade was a work of art, slightly longer than Roland's former sword. The long, straight blade glistened in the forge fire's glow, still red-hot as Horace prepared to harden it. As he dipped the blade into oil, the steam and fire it emitted rose in a sea of bluish-green smoke and flame. When he pulled the blade out, its colors became clear. Uniform patterns and folds flowed across the tang, bolster, cutting edge, and the blade itself. Blue and grey tones shimmered across the weapon. The flickering flames mirrored off its edge, revealing how sharp it already was even before touching the grindstone.

Horace set it down and retrieved a box that a craftsman had dropped off. Inside was the new handle for the weapon. The desert ironwood handle bore rich hues ranging from orange-yellow to deep red with streaks of brown. It had the original, beautiful pommel from the first sword, with one change: a small setting for a fragment of the stone that Horace had set aside. He had found it too beautiful to melt. He affixed it to the pommel and attached the handle to the sword.

Horace, his son, and Seoul looked at the finished weapon in astonishment. All three knew it was the finest work the blacksmith had ever done—and they also knew it was something special. They could feel it emanating from the sword.

The weapon was laid in the original box that the first sword had come in. Roland had kept the box safe over the years, and now it held something greater than before. Roland awoke the next day and, after spending some time with his queen and child, he headed down to the stables to tend to his horse. He knew the stable boy could do it, but he found it relaxing, and it helped clear his mind.

As he was brushing out his horse and feeding her sugar cubes, Horace and Thomas walked in.

"My king," Thomas said cheerily, "your weapon is ready."

Roland set down his tools and walked over to the nearby table, where Horace had set the box.

"I see you have refinished the box, Horace."

Horace smiled, proud that the king had noticed his work. "Yes, my lord. The woodsmith and I worked together. He sanded it down and put a new coat of varnish with ochre in it to bring out the color and seal it. I made a brand with your family coat of arms and burned it into the top. I also replaced the material inside with oiled leather where the blade sits and satin where the handle rests."

Horace opened the box, and Roland was amazed. He ran his hand along the desert ironwood handle, then up to the smooth center of the blade.

"Horace, my friend, again you have surpassed my expectations and created a piece of art. Thank you from the bottom of my heart."

The king reached around his back and pulled out two bags of gold, handing them to him.

"Lord, this is far too much!"

Roland smiled. "No, it is not enough for everything you do. And this sword may be what wins us the upcoming battle with Mathias."

"Thank you, lord," Horace said.

"Thomas, I'll meet with you later. We need to double our spies at the border. Mathias is definitely planning something, and we must be ready."

Thomas nodded, and he and the blacksmith walked away.

9

Roland, now alone, wrapped his hand around the hilt. He could feel a faint energy coursing through it. He assumed the meteor had integrated itself throughout the entire weapon. As he picked it up, he began to move it around, feeling how balanced it was, how right it felt in his hand. He swung the sword, practicing with it, and as he did, he felt the rock's power surge through him.

As he parried and sidestepped, a thin line of light began to run up and down his body, circling him in a bluish-purple, fire-like glow. It started at his feet and moved upward, creating an armor-like suit around him. Dark black boots appeared, fitted with metal shin and toe guards. Behind that came black, leather-like pants with metal thigh plates. As it rose, his torso was covered with a lightweight shirt, and chest, shoulder, and arm guards formed from nowhere.

At his neck, a long blue and purple cape unfurled from the shirt. When the light reached his head, a helmet appeared that matched the color and design of his new sword. The helmet rounded neatly around his head, with small wings protruding from each side. His family crest pushed itself up from the top and back. The glossy dark blue and grey patterns reflected even the smallest flickers of light, blindingly bright in all directions.

Roland realized his movements—his swings and thrusts—were faster and more precise. As he spun around, he sliced clean through the thickest beam holding part of the roof as though it were nothing. At that, he stopped. He was barely winded, impressed by the speed at which he had been moving.

But the thought made him worry: if Mathias had the same kind of power, then there would certainly be danger ahead. Mathias would not hesitate to seek revenge for every slight he believed he had endured in life.

The king laid the sword back in the box, and as he did, the suit of armor faded away. Roland stood still, confused at what had just happened. He picked up his belongings, re-stabled his horse, and headed back to the castle to speak with Thomas and Seoul.

10

Mathias awoke the next morning to find a large metal box sitting atop his coffer at the end of his bed. The heavy box was ash-grey, with a leather strip wrapped around the edges and fixed in place with large, rounded-head pins.

He opened it to reveal his twin axes lying back-to-back on a bed of dark red silk. As he picked them up, he felt the same kind of surge Roland had. The power buzzed through him.

He opened his door and beckoned to his guard.

"How may I help you, my liege?" the guard asked.

Mathias looked up with an evil grin. "Attack me."

The guard hesitated, confused and about to question the order. Mathias barked, louder this time: "Attack me, now!"

The guard lowered his halberd into position, preparing to strike—but before he could react, Mathias moved. At blinding speed, he rushed forward, axes in hand. As he did, a black metal suit, the color of cast iron, enveloped him.

The black light that circled him spun at dizzying speed, weaving itself into a fishnet-like metal suit. A helmet formed—slightly curved at the front with narrow eye slits—while the sides and back shimmered like overlapping fish scales, glimmering dark green, blue, and glossy black.

Before the guard could even complete his movement, Mathias was on him. He slashed down, then up, then inward from both sides. The man fell apart in nine pieces, collapsing like dead fish from a bucket. All that remained standing was one of the guard's legs. Blood pooled quickly, flowing into the cracks between the stone blocks of the floor.

Mathias was in awe of his weapons, his speed, and this new suit of armor. He admired himself and the axes, flicking them to throw the blood onto the floor. As he placed them back in the box, the suit and helmet dissipated into thin air. He knew that with these weapons and his army, he could regain the kingdom he believed had been stolen from him—and in the process, kill Roland once and for all. He grabbed the box and headed toward Megendra's sanctum. Passing a group of servants, he ordered them to clean up the mess in his room. The entire walk to the lower levels, he was planning his attack in his head.

11

Over the next couple of weeks, Roland doubled the border guards, scouts, and spies. While he strengthened his defenses, Mathias and Megendra plotted and schemed. Both sorcerers tried to spy on each other, but to no avail. From his past sessions with Seoul, Roland knew Mathias was working to create a weapon, though he did not know if he had succeeded. His gut told him he had, especially since spies reported increased activity along the border.

Thomas had been instructed to train the guards and re-train the veterans, with Seoul assisting. Seoul also prepared them against the kinds of magic they might face. Megendra did the same for Mathias's forces, though his training was brutal and violent, often leaving the chevaliers injured. Most of Mathias's men were not trained soldiers like Roland's. Many were common thieves—mostly street fighters—some conscripted into the feudal army for their crimes, and a few peasants accused of seditious remarks against the king. It was a police state. About a third of his men were archers, and of those, only half were even adequate.

12

About four weeks after Roland began training his troops and preparing them for the upcoming conflict, the day finally arrived. Three scouts raced in during the early evening and reported that Mathias and his army were on the move and would reach the border within a day or two. Roland met with all his soldiers in the war room to plan the battle. He knew Mathias was cunning and devious. As much as he hated to admit it, Mathias was also a skilled strategist. Thomas, Seoul, and Roland decided on a plan of action but knew they would need to be ready to adjust at a moment's notice. Everyone mounted up and headed to the border.

Roland carried his new weapon at his side and hoped Mathias hadn't figured out how to craft his section of the meteor into anything, but he was sure he had. Roland had known this battle was coming for years, though he hoped it would remain a normal fight without magic, especially magic they didn't fully understand.

13

Roland and his men met the other scouts and guards at the border. There was no sign of Mathias or his army. No sounds of troops. No torch lights. Nothing. The thick tree line ahead should have echoed any noise, and the night was dark with a new moon, meaning any light would shine through. The spot where the meteor had crashed was still a mess: hills of dirt shot up around the cavity left by its rough landing. The oddest part was the line at the border—a clear divide where Roland's side had begun to regrow grass while the other side remained dead. Nothing grew there; the dirt was black and lifeless.

Roland called up his scouts. "Where is the army? You said they would be here by now."

The lead scout, looking nervous, spoke up. "Lord, they should be. They were moving fast enough that we predicted they would be through the forest by now. We were worried they may have crossed the border already."

14

As the scout finished his sentence, an arrow pierced his neck, spraying blood across the king's face. Suddenly, the sky lit up with an orange glow from both sides. Flaming arrows reached their peak and began their descent.

"Shields up! We've been ambushed!" Roland shouted.

Most of the men managed to get their shields up in time. Fire and normal arrows rained down, piercing some shields while others struck the ground. Some of the fire arrows hit surrounding trees, igniting them, while others struck soldiers who failed to cover themselves or lacked shields, setting their bodies ablaze. The men who were hit ran screaming before succumbing to the fire that engulfed them. Seoul used his magic to form an invisible shield around himself and his king.

As the last barrage of arrows landed, Mathias' men charged from the woods—swords, hatchets, and halberds swinging in their hands. A few soldiers on horseback followed behind them with spears. The battle erupted. Mathias and Megendra sauntered out of the woods on their horses as the forest behind them flared into a growing wildfire, the flames ravenously devouring the trees. Roland and Mathias locked eyes. Roland drew his sword, and his armor formed around him once again. Mathias grabbed his axes, and the same transformation occurred.

132

Just as Roland started toward Mathias, a halberd flew at him, aimed to pierce his heart. On impact with the king, it shattered into pieces, exploding into shards. Roland realized none of these weapons could harm him. Two of his guards rushed Mathias, axes ready to slice him to pieces. Mathias hurled both of his axes at them, decapitating them and spraying blood everywhere as their bodies dropped. Like boomerangs, the axes returned to their owner.

Seoul shouted an incantation and hurled a long, bright white lightning bolt at Mathias. Its white-hot tail hissed steam as it cut through the air, but it lost power before reaching him and dissipated. Seeing this, Megendra followed with a magical dagger, glowing with black light as it zipped toward Roland. Just before striking him, the dagger veered sharply downward and buried itself to the hilt in the root of a tree.

At that moment, all four men understood the truth: mortal weapons and sorcery were useless.

15

Roland and Mathias rushed each other. In the arena of combat, valor and steel collided as they met. Mathias' twin axes clashed against Roland's sword, each weapon carrying its own legacy, each enchanted with its own rhythm in the deadly dance. Mathias, muscles taut, wielded his two gleaming axes with a symphony of brutality. Each axe, perfectly balanced for speed and power, hungered for Roland's flesh. The twin blades spun like a tempest of steel, their relentless bite seeking gaps in armor, rending shields, and sundering bone.

In that instant, both men realized that only they could harm each other. Mathias thrived in the chaos of close combat. He grinned, eyes aflame with the fury of all he believed Roland had stolen from him, and hacked toward his enemy with primal rage.

Roland defended the attacks, blade drawn. His sword, an extension of his honor, sang a different song—a song of grace and glory. The weapon arcs, tracing lines of destiny as sparks flew in every direction. They parried, deflected, and countered each strike. The edges, honed to a whisper, seek to pierce through armor and into flesh. The men's resolve was unwavering. Their lineage and the respect within their enchanted blades whispered memories of the past. They fought for survival, power, and legacy.

The men left their horses. Mathias lunged, axes descending like twin meteors. Sparks flew as they crashed against the sword's guard, both men moving at speeds no one had ever witnessed. The fire grew around them, unnoticed. Roland moved like a dancer—fluid and precise. His sword turned aside the swinging arcs, blocking and redirecting the axes. Locked in a struggle, they breathed the same air—Mathias' fury clashing with Roland's resolve.

Roland saw an opening. His blade pierced the physical armor, drawing first blood and finding the heart beneath. He pulled the sword free as Mathias grimaced and fell forward onto Roland's shoulder. Roland met his brother's eyes.

"You are defeated, brother. It is over."

Mathias, dying and gurgling blood, looked back and whispered, "I'll see you in hell."

Roland froze, confused. Mathias pushes himself off Roland's shoulder and, with a swift strike, sweeps the blades of his axes in an X pattern, slicing Roland's throat. As Mathias fell, a guttural laugh escaped his lips. His magical armor faded before his body hit the ground.

Roland dropped his sword and grabbed at his neck as blood spilled and sprayed, running down his chest and staining the ground. As soon as the sword hit the earth, his armor contracted into a small bubble at his chest and disappeared inside the king, like water down a drain. He turned toward Seoul and fell to his knees; his last sight was the worry in his friend's eyes.

16

While the brothers fought, Seoul and Megendra waged their own battle. Megendra summoned a mythical sword while Seoul enchanted his magical staff. Both fought fiercely. Seoul unleashed bursts of wind to throw Megendra back whenever he closed in. The staff held its own, blocking the maniacal swings of the sorcerer's sword.

When Seoul spotted a moment of weakness in Megendra's swings, the ball atop his staff sharpened to a deadly point. He plunged it deep into the man's stomach. Megendra's sword fell and dissolved into fog, blowing away with the wind. The victorious sorcerer lifted the wounded man with his staff and hurled him into a tree, driving the weapon deeper into his gut. Seoul uttered a few words, and iron shackles appeared, locking Megendra to the trunk. A metal strap melted across the sorcerer's mouth, his skin healing around it so he could cast no last-minute spells. As

Seoul walked away, the tree burst into flames, and the sorcerer disappeared into the unknown.

17

The fire was beyond control now. With Mathias dead, his men retreated. Many on both sides were already lost, many consumed by the flames. Seoul and Thomas ran to the king. They exchanged a glance and understood what needed to be done. Roland was too far gone for any medical or magical resuscitation. Thomas lifted the king and his sword, while Seoul grabbed Mathias and the axes. They hoisted the bodies onto their horses.

"Men! Retreat! Save yourselves and get back to the castle!"

The fire raged as Seoul, Thomas, and the surviving men—barely half of their number—leapt onto their mounts. They wove through the inferno, reigning in the horses this way and that, leaping burning logs until they finally broke free. They stopped and looked back at the forest. Animals fled in all directions, desperate to escape. They all knew the forest could not be saved. Their only hope was to keep the fire from spreading toward the castle. In silence, they rode back, their hearts heavy. Seoul cast a rain spell, hoping to douse the wildfire.

18

Word of the battle reached the castle before the party returned. The black smoke, darkening even the full moon in the sky, was visible across the entire island. The queen waited near the gate when the riders entered. She saw her king, her husband, draped lifeless across Thomas' horse. She ran forward and cupped his face, pressing her own to his. Her tears streaked his dirt-, sweat-, and soot-stained cheeks, leaving pale trails across his lifeless skin.

Once they reached the stables, Thomas removed the king and laid him on an empty wagon cart at the entrance. Queen Ami composed herself as best she could and asked Thomas what had happened. Thomas explained the battle while Seoul filled in the magical details.

Ami said, "He told me of the magic the stone held and that he was going to harness it, but I didn't know the extent of it."

Seoul wrapped a long arm around her. "He fought valiantly and, in his death, he saved the kingdom. You will have to decide what to do now that Mathias is dead—whether to reunite the entire kingdom or leave it as it is. Those decisions can wait. First, we must figure out how to properly bury the king and, unfortunately, his brother. The magic within them and their weapons must be safeguarded so no one can use them for evil again."

Tears streaked Ami's face. "Should we cremate them?"

Seoul stroked his beard, thinking. "I'm not sure that would work. It took deep magic to burn hot enough to shape the meteor. Now that the magic is within them, it may take a blaze hotter than my magic can create."

"What do you suggest?" Ami asked. "As much as I don't want them buried together, I understand it may need to be done."

"I think the best plan is to dig the cave on the eastern shore deeper and bury them there. Afterward, I'll cast a protection spell so no one can unearth them," Seoul said.

Ami agreed reluctantly. "Let it be done, then."

She called Thomas and several soldiers. "Please carry my husband inside. I want time for my daughter and me to say goodbye before I prepare him for burial."

The soldiers, along with Thomas, did as asked and carried the king into a room off the infirmary. A few minutes later, the queen and the princess entered to begin their final farewell.

19

Seoul worked with Thomas and many of the men in the castle on the plan for the burial. Twenty men made their way to the Whispering Cave, named for the eerie sounds that echoed from it when the westerly wind picked up. The cave sloped downward for about a hundred and fifty yards, then twisted back toward the direction of the castle and continued even deeper. After the first fifty or so yards, the opening narrowed. Seoul instructed the men to widen both the entrance and the path enough for the coffins to be brought inside. Once that was done, he asked them to go another two hundred yards past the point where the tunnel curved back.

It took about eight weeks to complete the work. Crews labored day and night until they struck a rock wall they could not break through, close to where they had planned to stop. The men laid logs against the rock, covering three of the four walls and part of the opening. All the stones they had

138

removed were piled in front of the cave entrance. The Whispering Cave was finally ready for its new inhabitants.

20

On the day of the funeral, the King's casket was transported in a decorated wagon cart. Lace and satin draped the wagon, shining brilliantly under the blazing sun. The Queen and her daughter rode in the front wagon, ahead of the King's coffin. Behind them came an older, plain wagon carrying the casket of Mathias. It bore no decorations and was accompanied only by its drivers.

After the two-mile trek to the Whispering Cave, both caskets were unloaded. Roland's was opened so Ami could say her final goodbye. She laid a piece of satin on the hand that held his sword to his chest, and his daughter placed a lily beside his arm. Ami whispered to Roland's still form, "Your legacy will not die with you. I am with child and pray to the gods it's a boy. Please watch over us, my love. I will see you in the afterlife."

Both caskets were identical in construction, made of dark brown mahogany and bound with iron straps that ran around the top and sides in an L-shape. Large iron nails sealed the lids to ensure they could never be opened. Roland's coffin bore beautiful carvings with gold and silver inlay and large, rounded decorative nails. Mathias's was engraved with protective runes to keep his evil contained and was already nailed shut, though without ornamentation.

Thomas and three of the King's men carried Roland to his final resting place, each offering a prayer as they set the box down. They then climbed back up to retrieve Mathias's

139

casket. Seoul accompanied them, chanting spells as they carried the man down. Only a single protective prayer for their own safety was spoken as they laid him to rest. Large wooden logs were stacked at the opening to seal the chamber. After everyone exited, the stones and boulders removed during excavation were used to close the cave's mouth.

Seoul ordered everyone to return to the castle except Ami and Thomas. Turning to Ami, he said, "I have a spell that will keep anyone from seeing or unearthing the cave until the end of time." Ami nodded. "Go ahead."

The sorcerer opened a book in one hand and raised his staff with the other. He cast a spell that bound not only the physical entrance of the cave but also tethered its closure to the very flow of time and cosmic energy—a spell both wondrous and intentionally fragile. "Tempus, fortis, apertum nullus!" he intoned.

A circle of ancient runes, shimmering with stardust, flared to life around a ring of enchanted monoliths at the cave's mouth. The runes, etched in a forgotten language that evoked the elemental power of earth and the relentless march of time, bound stone and shadow together, creating a barrier no mortal force could penetrate. "This cave will not be able to be seen or unearthed by any mortal being," Seoul declared. "The Cave of Whispers is now the Valley of Whispers."

The crystal ball atop his staff began to glow, emitting a jagged blue light that stabbed into the ground and then burst outward, encircling the cave. Before their eyes, the cave seemed to flatten and vanish, transforming into a broad valley—parts of it lush with grass, others dry and desolate. The memory of the cave was erased from everyone except the three who stood there, as a black-and-blue light shot upward and exploded, raining down over the entire island and altering every mind. Little did anyone know Megendra was casting his own spell and guarding his mind from the spell.

The three mounted the horses left for them and rode back to the castle.

Six months later, a baby boy was born to the Queen. She named him Prince Roland Thomas of Atheria, honoring both his late father and the man who had mentored him.

PART THREE
HISTORY & DESTINY

Present day:

Las Vegas Nevada SEMA show

1

On a crisp November morning in Las Vegas, Ronin wiped down his fully custom 1968 Hellaphant-powered Dodge Charger, making sure all his cars were ready before SEMA opened in a few hours. Ronin was a big man—6'5", 220 pounds, covered in tattoos. Short dark hair matched his dark eyes and olive complexion.

He had brought his four best vehicles: the Charger he was finishing now, a custom wide-body 1998 twin-turbo Honda Prelude, a fully built 2024 wide-body Ram 1500 twin-turbo Cummins diesel, and his one-of-a-kind stretched Vulcan motorcycle. Each had undergone extensive body work, plush interior upgrades, wild paint, and massive horsepower builds. No detail was overlooked.

His company, Atheria Customs, had been passed down from his adoptive father, who was actually his uncle. Ronin's parents had died during a virus accidentally released from a lab in Taiwan, a tragedy that became a scar in American history. Once his parents were put on ventilators, it was over. His aunt and uncle found him alone in his parents' apartment and adopted him. From then on, he spent every free moment in the shop with his uncle Alex and the crew.

Ronin's adoptive brother, Marcus, was about the same age, but from the start, he resented what he saw as an intruder in his home. Spoiled and entitled, Marcus never shared his father's passion for cars, motorcycles, and trucks. He showed up at the shop only to appease Alex, while Ronin immersed himself in the craft. After graduating, Ronin attended WyoTech to refine his skills, then returned to the shop to begin his career. He also took an interest in the business side, learning the company's operations inside and out. A gifted craftsman and shrewd businessman, Ronin seemed destined for the work, which only fueled Marcus's bitterness.

When Alex retired, he announced that Ronin would take over the business. At the board meeting where this was revealed, Marcus attacked his father. Ronin intervened, holding him off until security arrived. Marcus was banned from the building and the shop. He vowed to ruin Ronin and kill him. Over the years, he tried, even sabotaging Ronin's Porsche Carrera GT by cutting its brake lines. Ronin and his crew stayed vigilant.

As Ronin finished wiping down the last of his vehicles, his best friend and mentor Tommy arrived. Tommy, about fifteen years older but still youthful in spirit, was a 5'10" black man with a medium build and a few tattoos on his forearm. The two had met at Alex's shop when Ronin was a teenager, and Tommy had taken him under his wing.

"Tommy, nice time to show up. I just finished getting everything ready," Ronin said with a laugh and a smile.

"Then I showed up just in time," Tommy replied, grinning as they slapped hands and exchanged a bro hug.

2

Together, they began setting up their booth with T-shirts, hats, pamphlets, business cards, and photos of past builds. Their location near the entrance was ideal: visitors would see their vehicles first when entering and last when leaving, and merch sales were always stronger at the exit. Neither of them knew that Marcus and his crew—Johnny and Gavin—had used a few connections to secure this prime spot for Ronin. Their real reason was more sinister: it gave them the perfect chance to ambush the men and sabotage their showcase.

When the event opened, a large crowd gathered around the vehicles, admiring every detail. Some asked to hear the engines run, and the men obliged. Ronin fired up the Charger, its Hellaphant engine roaring with a low, raspy growl that shook the body. Tommy lit up the Vulcan, drawing cheers as the chrome and paint gleamed in the sunlight. Next came the Prelude, which gave the familiar Honda sputter before settling into a smooth idle. Though quieter, it sounded crisp; when Ronin purged the nitrous system, the sharp whoosh made the import fans ooh and ahh. Finally, the Ram thundered to life, compound turbos howling as black smoke rolled from the exhaust and the diesel engine thumped with power. The crowd erupted in excitement, and Ronin and Tommy felt confident the day would be a huge success.

But trouble was already moving in. Gavin slipped through the crowd and began causing a ruckus at the merch booth, drawing attention. When Ronin and Tommy rushed over to calm the situation, Marcus and Johnny made their move. Marcus, knowing the Charger was Ronin's favorite, jumped into it while Johnny climbed into the Ram.

The crowd murmured in confusion as Gavin bolted. Doors slammed. Tires squealed. Johnny stomped the gas, smashing through the crowd-control barrier and scattering people in every direction. Marcus followed close behind as both vehicles shot onto Paradise Road and then turned onto South Joe West Brown Street, heading toward East Sahara Avenue.

Ronin instantly knew who was behind the theft and why. He sprinted to the Prelude, fired it up, and tore out in pursuit, all four wheels spinning as the all-wheel-drive car clawed for traction. He drifted hard onto Paradise Road, tires screaming.

Tommy, startled at first, shouted, "Shit! Everyone move, get out of the way!" He leapt onto the Vulcan, spun it around in a haze of tire smoke, and roared after the thieves— determined to catch up with Marcus, Johnny, and Ronin.

3

At the same time, in the Hawaiian Islands (once known as the island of Atheria before separating after a massive earthquake), the Whispering Cave began to reappear. The ancient spell that concealed it was weakening. All the safeguards and restrictions Seoul had woven into the magic were reaching their limits.

The world stood on the brink of transformative energy surges—unforeseen electromagnetic shifts, quantum technological experiments, and peculiar cosmic alignments. Megendra, in the shadows, had designed a deliberate vulnerability into the spell. The intricate lattice of runes and temporal energies was meant to decay when certain cosmic and technological conditions arose. As advanced technology interacted with ley lines and rare celestial events tipped the balance of magical forces, the very weave of the enchantment began to fray.

Under these conditions, the seal faltered, its energy flickering like a candle flame caught by a sudden gust, allowing the cavern's secrets to seep outward. Seoul had crafted the barrier so the cave would remain hidden only until a destined convergence of fate and modern forces. It was both a safeguard and an invitation: when the appointed time arrived, a worthy heir or intrepid soul would witness the unraveling of the spell, proving that every lock has a key and every sealed mystery its moment to be revealed.

One by one, the locks broke. The flat land rose, the rocks sealing the cave crumbled, and the magical carvings faded more each day. At last, the final lock gave way. The mouth of the cave yawned open as the last stones fell. Terrified witnesses screamed and fled. The spell was completely broken.

Inside, both caskets erupted. Two lights flared in the darkness—a dark-blue sphere outlined in silver and a blood-red sphere shrouded in purple. They clashed violently, battling for dominance before shooting skyward, streaking toward the United States, where the descendants of Roland

and Mathias now lived. Over the twelve hundred years since their deaths, Roland's bloodline had spread across the world before settling in America. Few knew of the many illegitimate children Mathias had fathered, but one survivor remained—just as cruel and ruthless as Mathias himself.

4

Meanwhile, Ronin was closing in on Marcus. The Charger was fast, but the Prelude's speed and agility let it weave through traffic more easily than the Ram or the Charger. The chase tore off East Sahara Avenue onto Interstate 15 North, then quickly looped onto I-15 South. Construction had heavy traffic, but there was still enough space to maneuver. Tommy trailed far behind, slowed by security and police interference at the convention center.

Marcus and Johnny were about three miles past Martin Luther King Boulevard when Ronin caught up. Johnny spotted him first and grabbed his Motorola phone, using the walkie-talkie feature to warn Marcus.

"Yo, Marcus—look behind you. We've got company," Johnny said.

Marcus checked his rearview mirror and saw his brother's Prelude closing fast. "Let's see what these cars can do, Johnny," he cackled over the line.

Johnny floored the Ram, clearing a path with the truck's custom steel bumper and bull bar. Black smoke billowed from the compound turbos as the truck plowed forward, shoving two cars into the concrete median. Vehicles ahead swerved to escape, some making it, others clipped and scraped aside as the black steel carved through traffic.

Marcus stayed tight on Johnny's tail. Their speed climbed past ninety and rising.

Ronin matched them, his Prelude nimble enough to dodge the wreckage ahead. He caught Marcus and tried to spin the Charger by bumping its rear quarter panel, but Marcus anticipated the move. He swerved, braked hard, then accelerated away. The tactic battered the Charger's rear end; continued abuse would blow the back wheels if he wasn't careful.

"Find us a way out of here—we need to lose him!" Marcus shouted into his phone.

"Follow me, boss. I got you," Johnny replied.

Focused on each other, neither Marcus nor Ronin noticed the upcoming construction zone down to one lane. Only Johnny caught the orange warning signs flashing by. Seeing the next exit and the concrete barriers narrowing the highway just beyond it, Johnny yanked the wheel right and shot down the ramp.

Marcus nearly missed it, swerving hard to follow. The Charger's rear lost traction and smashed into the guardrail. Overcorrecting, Marcus sent the car sideways; the rim caught the asphalt, and the vehicle began to flip.

5

At that instant, the racing orbs reached the men. The dark-red sphere intercepted Marcus mid-flip, wrapping him in a cocoon of swirling energy as the Charger tumbled, crushing metal with every roll.

The blue sphere streaked into Ronin just as he approached the exit. He hadn't seen the lane closures in time.

Slamming his brakes, the Prelude dove nose-first into the concrete barrier and flipped end over end. The blue energy enveloped Ronin, suspending him inside a glowing cocoon.

The car's roof struck a parked construction truck before sliding sideways over the overpass. An oncoming tractor-trailer carrying a shipping container passed beneath at that exact moment, ripping the Prelude's front end clean off and hurling the rest of the car to the ground below. The battered shell rolled several times before spinning to a slow, finally stopping against the concrete pillar.

Johnny came running over to the car Marcus was in. With a sudden explosion, the door flew off, and Marcus stepped out without a scratch.

"Holy shit, Marcus, you're alive!" Johnny shouted.

Marcus patted himself down and yelled, "Let's get the fuck out of here!"

The two ran to the Ram and took off.

Tommy arrived just in time to see the Prelude fly into the air. "Oh no, Ronin," he said aloud. He twisted the throttle and sped toward the accident, taking the exit ramp. At the bottom, he saw a crowd of people running toward the wreck. One person was already spraying the car with a fire extinguisher.

Tommy parked the bike and ran to the mangled vehicle. As he reached it, the windshield shot out with a loud bang and slammed against the other underpass column. Ronin crawled out slowly. Tommy rushed over to help him.

Ronin wasn't bloody or bruised—not even a scratch.

"How the hell did you survive that? Your car is in two pieces, and one looks worse than the other!" Tommy said in shock.

Ronin looked around at the destruction, amazed he was still alive, but knowing something had saved him—though he didn't know what.

"I guess my guardian angel called in all the favors on that one," he said.

Tommy shook his head. "I guess we need to wait for the police and explain what happened." He let out a sigh.

The police arrived a few minutes later, along with firefighters and ambulances—none of which were needed. Tommy took the bike back to the convention center, loaded it, then returned with the car hauler to collect what remained of the two vehicles. The police took Ronin to the station for a statement and handed him a stack of tickets: speeding, reckless driving, driving an unlicensed/unregistered car, and property damage. Witnesses, however, backed him up, saying he hadn't started the chase.

6

Ronin and Tommy finally got back in the truck, trailer in tow, and began the twenty-six-hour drive home.

After eight hours, they stopped in Salt Lake City. Both men were dirty, exhausted, and still reeling from the day's events. They cleaned up, ordered Grubhub, and sat in silence until the food arrived.

Once they sat down to eat, Tommy finally broke the quiet.

"What in the actual hell happened back there? Racing after them was dumb, and you could have been killed! I honestly thought you were dead when I saw the car. You've got something—or someone—watching over your dumb ass."

Ronin, in the middle of a bite of lo mein, set down his chopsticks and took a moment to compose himself.

"I have no clue what happened. I'm used to Marcus messing with me, but I never thought he'd go this far. I was so blindingly mad I didn't see the signs, and before I knew it, I was upside down."

Tommy studied him. "I don't know how you didn't die. Between the concrete and the semi, anyone else would have been dead."

Ronin nodded slowly. "The weird thing is, once I slammed on the brakes, it felt like something wrapped me up, and I was in complete darkness. Next thing I knew, I was crawling out of the car."

Tommy just shook his head and went back to eating.

"Ronin, what's with the necklace? Did you just pick that up at a gift shop or something?"

Ronin ran his fingers over it. It was a silver herringbone chain with a pewter sword that almost looked like a cross, decorated with gold inlays and carved runes.

"I have no clue where it came from or how I got it," he admitted.

Tommy laughed. "Maybe the cute EMT nurse gave it to you for all we know."

Ronin shook his head and finished eating.

"I guess we should hit the hay. We've got a long couple of days ahead."

They threw out their trash and went to bed.

7

That night, Ronin woke up and found himself standing in a castle. His father sat on a throne, a knight at his side.

"You need to finish this, Ronin," his father said. "Or he will be the end of us—and hurt as many people as he needs to in order to get to you."

A noise sounded behind him. Ronin turned to see a man resembling Marcus charging forward, twin axes in hand. Ronin raised his sword, but wasn't controlling his own body. The man struck, knocking him down.

Ronin jolted awake with a heavy thump—he had fallen out of bed, dripping with sweat. It was ten minutes to four. He'd wanted to rise early, but this was ridiculous.

He stumbled into the bathroom, splashed water on his face, and looked into the mirror. Behind him stood the same knight from his dream.

Startled, he spun around, but nothing was there. He splashed more water on his face and looked again. This time, only Tommy was behind him.

"You okay, man? You look like shit," Tommy mumbled, half awake.

Ronin wiped his face with a towel. "Yeah, fine. Just had a weird dream. I'm getting dressed so we can leave—maybe we'll make it home by tomorrow if we're lucky."

152

8

About half an hour later, the two men hopped back into the truck and began another long day of driving. They talked about fixing the vehicles and how much it sucked to miss out on SEMA, promising each other they'd come back harder next year. But Ronin's mind kept drifting to the face of the knight he'd seen in his dream—and again in the mirror. The face felt familiar. Maybe he'd seen it in another dream, a nightmare, or even a book as a child.

The other man—the one attacking him—was also familiar, though Ronin couldn't figure out where or how he knew him. Maybe it was just a concussion from the accident, mixed with exhaustion and lack of sleep.

"Hey Tommy, can you drive for a bit? I think I might be having some side effects from the crash, and not sleeping isn't helping," Ronin said.

He pulled into the next rest stop, and they switched seats.

"You okay, man?" Tommy asked.

"Yeah, I'll be okay," Ronin replied. They drove for sixteen hours that day, switching back and forth so one could sleep while the other drove. Eventually, they stopped at a small roadside motel—cheap and about eight hours south of home. For dinner, they crossed the street to a Bojangles, choosing it simply because it was close. Both ordered chicken sandwich meals and shared some chicken tenders.

9

As they were leaving, they saw an older man being harassed by a younger man who looked strung out on drugs. The younger man shoved the older man to the ground.

Ronin didn't hesitate. He ran toward them.

"HEY, HEY! Leave the old guy alone! What the fuck is wrong with you?" he shouted.

He leaned down to help the older man, but the younger man suddenly pulled a gun. Without even thinking—or truly knowing what was happening—Ronin snatched the elderly man's cane. He spun it like a sword, striking the gun and knocking it out of the attacker's hand. He swept the cane behind the man's knee, dropping him, then delivered a sharp strike to the jaw, sending the assailant flying backward and leaving him unconscious in the parking lot.

Ronin handed the old man his cane and the wallet he had dropped. Tommy ran over to help the man to his feet. After making sure he was safe and on his way, Tommy turned to Ronin.

"What the fuck, man? Do you have a death wish? That crackhead had a gun!"

"I don't know what just happened. It was like… something took over," Ronin said, confused.

"Whatever it was," Tommy laughed, "it was badass. Where'd you learn those moves? You swung that cane like it was a sword."

"I seriously don't know. I could see everything happening but couldn't control it," Ronin admitted, a worried edge to his voice.

"You must've hit your head harder than we thought in that crash. I guess I'll finish the driving tomorrow. Let's get back to our room before more trouble shows up."

The two returned to their room, showered, and went to bed.

10

That night, Ronin dreamed again—but this time he was aware and ready. His father repeated the same warning. Again, the mysterious attacker appeared, swinging at him. This time, Ronin defended himself. Sparks flew as their weapons clashed, and the force of it pushed him out of the dream.

He woke with a jolt, shielding his eyes as he sat up. Sweat soaked his clothes. It took a few seconds to remember where he was. Dripping wet, he got up and went to the bathroom to shower, refusing to look in the mirror in case the mysterious figure appeared again. Instead, a faint voice whispered in his head. He couldn't quite make out the words—it was like a distant echo in a dream. But he thought it said, "We need to palavar."

11

While Ronin and Tommy continued their drive home, Marcus and Johnny were preparing to board a plane. Marcus looked terrible—he hadn't been sleeping either. Nightmares plagued him: visions of being bested by some rogue warrior, stabbed in the chest, dying, and being trapped in some unknown place.

He didn't know who the man in his dreams was, but the face felt familiar. And deep inside, Marcus felt a burning hatred for him. The nightmares had eased slightly, but the feeling of betrayal and rage lingered.

The only thing that brought Marcus a shred of satisfaction was knowing he had ruined Ronin's SEMA debut. Ronin had probably lost his invitation for future shows, and the damage to his vehicles would cost him dearly. But Marcus still couldn't understand how Ronin had survived the crash—or how he himself had. The details of the accident were a blur.

His revenge was far from complete. This, he thought, was only the beginning.

"Loading for Flight 1928. First class, disabled persons, and military veterans may now board," came the announcement over the loudspeaker.

Johnny tapped Marcus. "That's us, boss. Let's go."

Marcus snapped out of his thoughts and followed Johnny to the board. He decided that he and Johnny would sit separately, and Gavin would drive back, just in case they were identified. As far as anyone knew—including Ronin—they hadn't been.

Marcus settled into his first-class seat, turned on the in-flight television, and soon drifted into uneasy sleep, where his dreams took over.

12

Marcus awoke inside a dimly lit cave, searching for the source of a faint glow. As he moved closer, he saw a man in a long hooded robe holding a staff topped with a crystal that pulsed with light.

Marcus recoiled. "This is just a dream. I need to wake up."

The figure stepped forward.

"This is no dream. You can fight it all you want," the man said, his voice echoing. "I am Megendra, your ancestor's greatest mage and counselor. Mathias—the rightful king of Atheria—was killed by the usurper Roland, the bastard prince."

As Megendra spoke, shimmering images appeared around the cave walls, replaying scenes of a final battle.

Marcus stepped closer, eyes wide. "I've seen this in my dreams! That's the man I always see attacking me. Who is he?!"

"These are not dreams, but memories of your ancestor," Megendra said. "His body and soul were imprisoned by a curse. The curse has been broken, and now Mathias's soul resides within the talisman around your neck. The man you recognize is Roland—the usurper I spoke of."

Marcus reached under his shirt and pulled out the necklace. It glowed faintly purple.

"I can feel the hatred within you," Megendra continued, "the hatred for a man who resembles Roland. That is because he is his descendant. Your enemy is the blood of your ancestors' enemy. Both are tyrants. Both must be destroyed. Your bloodline must be avenged."

Marcus clenched the necklace in his fist. "I've tried taking him out, but he always survives."

"There is a way. You can let Mathias live inside you. His magic and skill can help you seek your revenge. All you need to do is summon him, setting him free from the talisman."

Marcus looked spooked. "I'm not giving up my body for anyone! I know how this goes, I've seen the movies —I'll be trapped in my body with no control!"

The ghostly figure studied him for a second before speaking. "You will have full control of your body. The only changes will be your skills, the magic you will possess, and the ability to speak with the rightful king as if he is there with you—a consciousness in your mind."

Marcus froze, unsure what to do. He turned to walk away, but after a few steps, Megendra appeared in front of him again. Every direction Marcus tried, he managed only a few steps before the magician blocked his path. There was no escape.

"Fine!" Marcus yelled. "How do I release him?"

Megendra gave a sickly, sinister smile and pointed his staff at Marcus. "Hold the talisman in your hand and repeat after me: ego dimittam te et dabo tibi vitam."

Marcus repeated the incantation. Megendra's wand glimmered dark purple, the energy swirling around the gem in his staff. After a few seconds, it shot into Marcus's chest, surrounding the necklace and then spreading to his hands before enveloping his entire body. The dark glow brightened suddenly and blasted Marcus backward.

Marcus woke up screaming and flailing, startling the nearby passengers. Flight attendants rushed over to assist him. He pushed them away at first, then came out of his fog and realized he was on a plane. Embarrassed, he assured the stewardesses he was fine—it had just been a bad dream.

As the cabin settled, Marcus thought back to his nightmare. It felt too real to dismiss. Deep down, he felt…different. He wasn't ready to admit it, but something inside him had changed.

13

While Marcus was dreaming and his hatred growing, Ronin and Tommy were just getting back to the shop well after midnight. Both were tired and sore. They pulled the rig into the garage, locked up, and after a few quick goodbyes, went their separate ways.

Ronin arrived home to see Amy's car in the driveway. Relieved to be back, he unlocked the door and found her asleep on the couch. He covered her with a blanket, then lay down on the other couch and quickly drifted off.

This dream was different. Ronin stood in the castle again, but everything and everyone were frozen, like a paused video game. Looking down, he saw armor on his wrists, hands, and—on closer inspection—his entire body. Confused, he wondered if he was dreaming.

"Welcome back," a low voice said as a hand landed on his shoulder.

Startled, Ronin spun around with his fist raised. The voice's owner lifted a calming hand. "There's no need to be frightened. If I intended harm, I would have struck while your back was turned."

For reasons he couldn't explain, Ronin felt a strange calm at the sight of the robed man, even though the hood hid his face. It was as if he somehow knew him.

"I understand your confusion," the man said, lowering his cowl to reveal his face. "This is no dream, my friend. I am here to explain the voices and the visions."

He leaned on the stone railing. "This was the beginning of the end for your ancestor, King Roland. This battle changed everything. I am Seoul, Roland's mage, friend, and counselor."

Ronin found himself relaxing more with each word. He leaned on the railing as well. "But what does any of this have to do with me? Why involve me after more than two centuries?"

Seoul regarded him carefully, placing a hand on Ronin's shoulder before waving his other hand. The frozen scene around them sprang to life, the battle unfolding before Ronin's eyes until the banishment of Mathias.

"Does any of this seem familiar?" Seoul asked.

Ronin thought about everything that had happened with Marcus over the years.

"History repeats itself, my son," Seoul said, reading his thoughts. He waved his hand again, showing the final battle, the burial of Roland and Mathias, and the casting of the protection spell.

"Unfortunately, the spell has been broken. Roland's spirit is entombed in the necklace you now wear. I'm certain Mathias and Marcus have been speaking with Megendra. I fear they plan to kill you—to take revenge on the descendants of those who wronged them. That descendant, Ronin, is you."

Ronin paced, struggling to absorb it all. "Marcus has been trying to take me out for years. He's always failed, and he won't succeed now."

"The problem," Seoul said gravely, "is that if Megendra frees Mathias inside Marcus, Marcus will possess all the powers, memories, and magic Mathias died with."

Ronin's face tightened. "So what am I supposed to do? How can I protect my family—and myself—from that?"

Seoul waved his staff. The castle vanished, leaving them in a dark room lit only by the glow of his staff. "You must do the same. Set your ancestor free from the pendant. Let him join your consciousness. He will guide and protect you, sharing his powers, memories, and magic."

Ronin sank to the floor, hoping this was just a nightmare but knowing it wasn't. Deep down, he felt he was meant for something greater.

"I don't know if I'm right for this," he admitted, standing again. "I don't know if I'm the one you want."

Seoul locked eyes with him. "You are the one we need. This is your destiny. Only you can wield this power."

Ronin straightened, resolve hardening. "Let's do this."

He pulled the necklace free and held it out.

"Repeat after me," Seoul instructed. "Libera regem verum. Rex, in hunc, sua voluntate, mundum serva."

Ronin echoed each phrase. His hand opened involuntarily as the pendant sank into his skin like molten metal, glowing as bright as the midday sun until everything was blinded by light. The brilliance enveloped his outstretched hand and then his entire body.

14

Ronin woke in a heavy sweat with Amy shaking him awake. She was on her knees next to him, repeating his name like a mantra.

"Ro, wake up. Honey, wake up."

Ronin thrashed in confusion until his eyes finally focused on Amy. He sat up quickly, and she looked at him quizzically, trying to figure out what was going on.

"Just a bad dream, babe," he said, brushing the back of his hand along her petite jaw. For the first time in their relationship, Ronin lied to her.He knew it was more than a dream. In the back of his mind, he heard the familiar voice from the hotel, a whisper just above silence: We will palaver later.

Amy hugged him tightly. "Oh my god, when did you get home?" she asked, leaning into his hand. "I didn't hear you come in. I've missed you like crazy."

"I missed you too," Ronin said, kissing her hand. "I got home a few hours ago. You were sleeping so well, I didn't want to wake you."

She gave him a big hug and sat back on the couch. "So how was the show? I didn't think you'd be back this early."

Ronin explained everything, watching her expression tighten.

"What the hell, Ro? Why didn't you call me—or have Tommy call me?!" she said, her voice sharp with worry.

Ronin let out a long sigh. "I didn't want you to worry. I was safe, so it's all good."

She crossed her arms. "Why did you even go after him in the first place? He always goads you, and you always fall for it. He's hurt you before—you're lucky he didn't get you killed this time."

Ronin took a deep breath. "I know. Believe me, I do. But it's like I don't even think about it. It feels predestined, and I don't realize I'm doing it until it's done."

Amy softened a little. "I can't pretend to understand the dynamic between you two, but I don't want to see you get hurt because of his envy." She took both of his hands in hers.

"Amy, it kills me that he's trying to take Dad's company. He doesn't want to improve it—he just wants to take it because I earned it. I worked hard and learned the business. He wants to ruin me by ruining our father's legacy. I think that's why I go after him every… single… time."

Amy hesitated, then said quietly, "If you keep going after him, he'll get what he wants—either to ruin you or to kill you. He wins, not you."

Ronin took her words to heart. "You're right, as always," he said with a faint smirk. "I'll be more careful and cautious when I can. There will be times I can't be, but when I can, I will. I promise."

Amy gave him a hug and a soft kiss on the cheek. "Why don't we get some more sleep? When we wake up, we can go out for breakfast," she said, taking his hand and leading him to the bedroom.

They made love and fell asleep quickly afterward. Ronin knew, as he drifted off, that his ancestor would appear. Questions swirled in his mind, waiting for the moment they could meet.

15

Ronin wasn't wrong. Now that Roland was in his head, they were linked—awake or asleep.

He found himself sitting in a large oak chair with ornate carvings only a master craftsman could create. The seat was covered in a strange leather he had never seen, and the backrest was draped in a thick fur that looked like it had come from a wolf far larger than any he knew existed.

Before him stood a massive live-edge table, nearly round and full of beautiful knots, its surface stained a soft gray. He ran his hands across the smooth ridges of the grain, reassuring himself that it was real. Ten other chairs, each similar to his, ringed the table.

At the head sat the man Ronin had glimpsed in his recent dreams—someone who shared many of his features, marked by obvious battle scars and dressed in what looked like a gambeson, the padded garment worn beneath armor. Next to the man rested a sheathed sword, attached to his throne-like chair, and at his side lay a magnificent black-and-white dire wolf with piercing blue eyes.

"So, we finally meet and are able to palaver, Ronin, last of my ilk," the man said. "I have learned much about you since our minds and souls have bonded. Our lives are similar in their timelines. Fate and ill luck have brought us together. I am King Roland, ruler of Atheria."

Ronin sat in awe, still confused. "I am Ronin, king of none," he replied with a faint smile and chuckle.

Roland studied him for a moment before laughing. He rose from his seat and walked toward his descendant. "Let us walk and speak of what is happening. Now that our minds are one, I can show you everything. I know Seoul revealed much, but not everything."

Roland placed his hands on Ronin's head. Instantly, visions raced through Ronin's mind like a high-speed film—centuries of history compressed into seconds, yet perfectly clear, like a movie he had watched a million times. He understood everything: the birth of his ancestor, the rise and fall of kingdoms, and why Marcus and Mathias posed such a threat.

When Roland removed his hand, Ronin shook his head, absorbing the flood of knowledge. "Marcus has always been dangerous and cruel, but if he's united with Mathias, then we're in real trouble," Ronin said. "Other than killing me, what else could he want?"

Roland stood in thought. "He always sought to rule Atheria. But the world he inhabits now is much larger. I cannot say for certain what his ultimate endgame will be."

16

Marcus got home to his upscale house and tossed his bag onto the couch. Earlier, he'd met the boys at the bar and told them to lay low—go radio silent for a while.

He turned on the television, flipping through news channels to see if the chase had made local or national coverage. CNN carried only a small blurb about it on the ticker. That was it.

Satisfied, he got up and took a shower. When he stepped out, towel around his waist, he stood before the full-length mirror, checking for bruises or cuts from the accident.

Then it hit—like a bad acid trip.

The room dissolved, and suddenly he was in the sky, rocketing downward toward a massive castle. He plunged through the ceiling and walls like a ghost until he landed in a chamber, settling into a great ironwood chair covered in ornate leather.

Mathias paced the floor. His full black armor gleamed— embossed shoulder plates and beautiful gray body armor, every surface engraved with intricate markings.

Marcus stood abruptly. "What the fuck—you can't just do that. Your wizard or whatever says I have control!"

Mathias barely glanced at him. "We have no time for your bellyaching. We need a plan. I've seen much in your mind. This land has changed—far more sprawling than the one I was born to. We must kill off Roland's ancestor and begin by taking over this land. We need to raise an army."

Marcus scowled, torn between irritation and agreement. Ronin needed to be taken out once and for all. His anger outweighed his need to be respected. He sat back down. "So, where do we start? I can't raise an army, but I've got a crew who'll do what they're told—for the right price."

Mathias turned, finally giving him a full look. He could see the resemblance but thought his ancestor looked weak, both mentally and physically. "Price won't be an issue once we take this place you call a town. We'll need more as we spread."

Marcus smirked. "There are crews all over who'll take orders—my guys, others. Some want cash, some want power, some just want to watch the world burn."

Mathias shook his head. "Money and power are always craved. The ones who only want chaos—use them first. No great loss if they fall."

Marcus hesitated. "Do we know how connected Ronin and Roland are? Have they figured out how to link up like we have?"

"My best guess is yes," Mathias said, teeth clenched. "Ronin is resourceful, more than anything. If he's anything like Roland, we must be careful. I doubted him once before. That will not happen again."

"Fine," Marcus said. "I'll raise the army."

"Good. We'll palaver again later," Mathias replied, waving his hand.

Marcus felt himself ripped backward, flying out of the chamber and slamming back into his body—now sitting cross-legged in front of the mirror.

His rage flared. He drew back a fist to smash the mirror glass, and as he swung, a blade formed mid-air—molten black and white—along with a gauntlet that climbed his forearm and encased his hand. His punch shattered the mirror, the drywall, and even the stud behind it.

He pulled back, stunned. The gauntlet matched Mathias's armor—same dark sheen, same ornate markings.

The blade gleamed like chrome, black and white carvings spiraling along its length, a bright jewel set behind the knuckles.

Marcus turned his arm, inspecting it. After a few moments, the weapon retracted into his wrist, as if sliding back into his radial artery. He flexed his hand, twisting it to check for damage.

"You're learning," Mathias's voice echoed in his head.

Marcus smiled wildly as dark ideas coursed through his mind. He went to bed, already plotting his next move—recruiting more people, taking the streets, and luring Ronin out to test his powers before destroying him. Sleep came fitfully.

17

Morning broke with a hard edge. Marcus woke restless but with a plan. He climbed into his old truck and drove to Johnny's place, a sagging mobile home collapsing in on itself.

Johnny opened the door, surprised. "Hey, boss. What's up? Everything okay?"

Gavin stumbled out behind him, a joint dangling from his lips. He'd clearly been up all night getting high. "Hey, boss," he mumbled, collapsing onto a dilapidated couch.

"Get the rest of the guys together," Marcus said. "We're taking out Ronin for good—and starting to take the streets. Anyone who wants to get paid is in."

Johnny gave him a wary look. "What do you mean, take over the streets?"

Marcus smirked, Mathias's presence stirring inside him. "Let's just say we have a benefactor who wants this town—and maybe more. But first, Ronin must die."

Johnny shrugged. "Okay. I'll get our guys. Chavez's crew will do anything for money. Want me to reach out to LoSpecchio and his boys? They're crazy—vicious. They should all be locked up."

Marcus's smile widened. These were exactly the kind of people he needed to pull off his plan. Mathias's voice hummed approval. These were the fools he had once surrounded himself with.

18

Ronin was home alone while Amy was at work. He sat in front of the mirror, where Roland appeared like a faint specter in the reflection. They could communicate in Ronin's head, but this felt more natural.

"So, am I a superhero now?" Ronin laughed.

Roland tilted his head, confused by the word, then sifted through Ronin's mind until he found its meaning. He chuckled. "I do not think we will be fighting crime the way Batman or Spider-Man did. We will be more like Thor and Loki. We need to stop our brothers. I stopped Mathias once, but I am sure he will empower Marcus to commit some kind of crime—or help him kill you and me in the process."

Ronin thought for a second. "Marcus has already committed crimes and tried to hurt me. Escalating to murder isn't out of the question. Do I need a costume or disguise? Things are different now than they were in your time."

Roland probed through Ronin's memories again, pulling up his idea of a costume. "Stand up," Roland said.

From the necklace around Ronin's neck, a dark liquid began to pour out and flow over his body. The substance spread quickly, running over his chest, arms, and legs before solidifying. Ronin closed his eyes as the thick fluid covered his face. When he opened them, he was staring at a full Superman suit.

Ronin burst out laughing. "No way. People will think I'm some crazy guy in a Superman suit. Try again."

The black material loosened, turning back to a liquid that retracted and then flowed outward once more. This time, when it hardened and the colors settled in, Ronin was wearing the brown Wolverine outfit. He laughed even harder.

"Since you can dig through my thoughts, let me show you what I'm actually picturing," Ronin said. He closed his eyes and imagined something custom—protective but modern.

The necklace rested cool and unassuming against his chest. Then a pulse of light flickered from it, subtle at first, like a ripple spreading through water. The metal liquefied, spilling out in dark, snaking tendrils that slithered over his shoulders and down his arms. It moved like something alive—stretching, coiling—an intelligent tide pulling itself together.

The ooze thickened as it spread, clinging to his form and hardening in layers. The texture shifted from a viscous flow to an armored lattice, its surface rippling with emerging hexagonal scales. The air seemed to crackle as the transformation locked into place, the liquid metal setting into its final form: a seamless, protective armor.

Ronin flexed his fingers beneath it. The suit moved with him, impossibly light, breathing with each motion. Wrist guards and shoulder plates tightened into place. The headpiece sealed around his face, polarized eye slits sliding open. He exhaled slowly. The process was complete.

He tested it immediately. Grabbing a pair of scissors from the counter, he pushed the tip against the armor—nothing. He gritted his teeth and slammed the blades against his leg. The scissors bent.

Ronin pictured the mask retracting, and the liquid instantly flowed back down into the necklace. He looked at Roland in the mirror and grinned. "This is awesome. What else can it do?"

"Anything you can imagine," Roland replied with a sly smile. "Think of a sword and shield, and they will form. Go ahead—try it."

Ronin planted his feet and raised his forearm. A shield blossomed into existence in seconds. He cocked his other arm, and a sword grew from his wrist, solidifying in his hand just as quickly.

He lowered the shield, and it melted back into the suit. The sword followed. Ronin's grin widened as he met Roland's ghostly gaze.

"Next," Roland said, "I will show you the skills I learned. I think I can fold them into your thoughts. I am not certain how, but I will try."

Ronin felt a sharp jolt in his head, then a strange wobble—like his brain turning to Jell-O—before it passed. Roland stepped out of the mirror, still ghostlike.

They moved to the living room. "Show me what you have," Roland said, summoning a sword that solidified in his grip.

Ronin raised his arm, and a matching blade formed. The two swords clanged as they met. His mask reformed around his head as they began to spar. Steel rang through the room as they parried back and forth. Roland pressed the attack, forcing Ronin to retreat until Ronin suddenly brought up the shield. Roland's blade slammed against it. Seizing the moment, Ronin lunged, but Roland sidestepped. They continued, their movements mirroring each other almost perfectly.

The phone rang. Both froze.

Roland's armor opened at the back pocket, and he pulled out the device. Amy's name and photo lit the screen.

"Hi, babe, what's up?" Ronin answered.

"Hey, honey, the powder coater called," Amy said. "Your parts for the Monte Carlo are ready. I'm going to pick them up and drop them off at the shop, if that's okay. Both places are on my way home."

Roland—still smiling at Amy's support—replied, "Sure, I'd really appreciate that."

"It's all good," she said. "I'll be home about five. Gotta run. Love you."

"Love you too. Talk to you soon."

Ronin turned and noticed Roland was gone, along with his armor. He went back to the mirror and saw Roland waiting for him.

"I think you have the skills now. Hopefully, you won't need them, but with our brothers, I highly doubt it. Just keep your guard up."

Roland nodded. "I will."

As Roland began to fade away, his voice echoed inside Ronin's head: I'm here with you always. If you need me, just say my name in your consciousness, and I will answer.

Ronin showered and called Tommy to meet him for lunch to discuss plans for repairing the vehicles, the game plan for next year's SEMA, and getting back to work on customers' cars. After the call, Ronin stomped his foot and watched the armor appear instantaneously, then stomped again and saw it pull back into the necklace just as fast.

19

Meanwhile, Marcus was in his own run-down garage, alone, while the boys were out recruiting. Mathias appeared in front of him—more an apparition than flesh, his pale skin from his previous life adding to the unsettling sight.

"If all goes as planned, you'll need some sort of armor. If Ronin is anything like Roland, he will be formidable. The small piece of the stone in your necklace can form whatever you imagine—as you saw when you punched the mirror," the ghostly Mathias barked.

Marcus shot back angrily, "I don't need any armor against him. He doesn't scare me."

Annoyed by the man's tone, Mathias flicked the necklace with a ghastly finger, his touch passing through the pendant. The snake charm settled against Marcus's collarbone, cool and unassuming—until a simple thought stirred something inside it.

A quick bright pulse. A shift. Then the vines emerged.

Black vines crawled outward, slick and unnatural, curling over his skin like smoke caught in slow motion. They moved with purpose, spilling down his shoulders, wrapping around his arms and chest. This wasn't just a coating; the evil was claiming him. Layer by layer, the vines hardened. Scale patterns rose to the surface, locking together like an intricate puzzle, turning the vine-like threads into armor. It clung to his frame, tightening in precise movements and adjusting to the contours of his body.

His breath came ragged. He felt it flex around him—impossibly light yet solid, responding like a second skin. The last remnants of the plantlike climbers vanished, absorbed into the structure. The suit was seamless, resilient, ready. It looked as dark and menacing as the heart of the man inside it.

Once the suit formed, Mathias thrust his hand into Marcus's head. His ghostly fingers disappeared inside, and Marcus felt as if his brain were on fire—melting—as Mathias pushed his knowledge and skills into Marcus's psyche. The pain subsided, leaving Marcus with a strange, complete awareness.

When he finally looked up, a ghostly axe materialized in front of his neck. Without thinking, he jumped back.

Instinctively, he cocked both arms up and then down. In each hand, vine-like material formed into twin axes almost instantly, matching the ones Mathias held.

Marcus wasted no time and attacked the shadowy phantom. The axe sliced across Mathias's neck—but there was no resistance. The blade passed through the ghostly flesh. Marcus had swung so hard he stumbled forward, and when he regained his footing, Mathias's axe head was at his own throat, a thin line of blood beginning to trickle.

"I have given you my knowledge," Mathias warned. "Use it, or next time I will spill more than a drop of blood."

Marcus seethed but understood his ancestor's point. He steadied himself, digging into his thoughts. Once composed, he attacked again. This time, his movements matched Mathias's perfectly, like a well-choreographed dance. After about fifteen minutes of clashing, Mathias disappeared, though Marcus could still feel him inside his head. Together, they felt ready to put their plan into action.

Marcus returned to the office just as Johnny and Gavin came back with about five men from a few other crews and two members of the LoSpecchio gang. Gavin introduced them. "This is Gorgon—everyone calls him G—and this is Victor. I think you know everyone else."

Marcus shook their hands. "I've got a big job for you. Think you can handle it?"

The two men exchanged a look. Victor spoke, his voice low and gravelly. "As long as the money's there, we can handle anything."

Marcus smiled. "Money isn't an issue. Step into my office, and we'll talk." He turned to Johnny and Gavin. "All of you meet me at Ronin's shop around four. We're gonna finish this."

The men nodded and headed out while Marcus went into the room with the LoSpecchio boys and shut the door.

20

Tommy and Ronin were finishing their late lunch and business meeting when both their phones went off—the motion detector cameras at the shop. On the screen, they saw several people breaking in and trashing the customer vehicles outside.

Ronin dropped a hundred-dollar bill on the table, and they ran out the door. They jumped into Tommy's truck—a Ram 3500 with a custom paint job they'd done as a shop/show vehicle a few years earlier. Tommy screeched out of the parking lot and headed for the shop.

Mathias handed the crew a bag, and they piled into a 1979 Chevy Caprice before speeding off. Mathias and Marcus grinned, eager to see Ronin's reaction when the plan was complete.

Ronin and Tommy jumped out with bats and charged the crew Mathias had sent. Gavin hotwired the 1970 Monte Carlo while Johnny found the keys in the truck of the 1970 K30 and rammed through the garage door before taking off.

Ronin and Tommy fought the remaining few attackers until they scattered at the sound of approaching sirens.

Amy, seeing the camera alerts on her phone, immediately headed toward the shop.

While Ronin and Tommy fought the remaining five people, Victor and G slipped in through the back and pulled a few packs of C-4 Mathias had given them out of the bag. They placed one in each corner and the largest on a fifty-five-gallon drum of race gas. Setting the timers for seven minutes, they crept back out. Once in their car, they eased onto the street, pulling over to let the oncoming police cars scream past, sirens blotting out every other sound.

Amy arrived at the shop at almost the same time as the police. She pulled her Honda Pilot alongside the building, careful to avoid the broken glass and destroyed car parts. The police joined her, walking over to Ronin and Johnny.

The officers began their report. "Do you have proof of ownership or insurance on the building, sir?" Officer Whitney asked.

Amy spoke up, "I've got the insurance paperwork inside. I'll go grab it."

Ronin nodded. "I've got a bunch of paperwork over here in the shipping container."

As the men walked toward the container, Amy carefully made her way through the glass into the building. She headed to the filing cabinet for the insurance paperwork—then froze. A blinking light flickered behind the cabinet. She moved closer and saw the source: a timer, with seventeen seconds left.

Amy bolted out, screaming, "There's a bomb! There's a bomb!"

The men turned, realizing what she meant—

BOOM. BOOM. BOOM. BOOM.
BBBBOOOOOMMMMM—

The explosives detonated one after another, destroying all of the vehicles within the blast radius. The one on the gas barrel blew last, the largest explosion of all. Amy, mid-scream, was thrown into the air, flying through the air, and slammed down hard onto the pavement littered with car parts.

Ronin and the others sprinted toward her as the building erupted into a blazing inferno. The chemicals and cars inside went up in a chain of mini-explosions. Ronin shouted, "Call 9-1-1! Call 9-1-1!"

Amy's back was burned, her shirt and bra melted into her skin. A jagged piece of metal jutted from her hip. Ronin knelt, panicked, cradling her in his arms. "Get the fucking ambulance here—she's hurt!"

The officer spoke into his lapel mic, summoning an ambulance and fire crew. Tommy was already on his phone with 9-1-1. The sirens grew louder, closer.

Amy, her voice faint, looked at Ronin through half-lidded eyes. "I don't want to die. Who would do this?" Then she slipped into unconsciousness.

Ronin's heart burned with rage. He knew exactly who was responsible.

Inside his head, Roland whispered, heavy with regret: I should have killed Mathias when we were children. I am so sorry, Ronin.

Ronin answered silently, *We're* going to end this. I won't let him hurt anyone else.

The ambulance screeched to a stop. Medics rushed out, working quickly. They left the scrap metal in her hip to prevent bleeding out, then lifted her onto the gurney. Ronin kissed her before they wheeled her away.

21

The police taped everything off, and the firefighters started spraying the building. "Mr. Kastle, we'll need to talk more. Can you come to the station in the morning?" Officer Whitney asked.

Ronin muttered, "Yeah, whatever," and headed for the Bronco that Mathias's men had overlooked. The keys had been destroyed in the fire, so he popped the hood, stripped the ignition live wire, and connected it to the coil. He pressed the relay for the starter—the truck roared to life.

Tommy ran over. "What the hell are you doing?"

Ronin's head snapped toward him, eyes blazing. "Marcus went too far this time. I'm done with this shit. He's mine."

Tommy jumped into the passenger seat.

"Get out, Tommy. This isn't your fight." Ronin didn't want him discovering his new secret; he doubted his friend could handle it.

"You're not going there alone. He's probably got all his guys with him."

Ronin sighed. "Fine. Let's go."

They sped toward Marcus's run-down garage. The weather shifted as if it knew what was coming. Clouds

179

thickened, grew darker. The first drops of rain fell, heavy and cold, a storm gathering on the horizon.

Ronin and Tommy sped toward Marcus's garage.

"I need to tell you something. Show you something," Ronin said, eyes locked on the road.

Tommy glanced at him curiously. "I don't like the sound of that. Last time you said that, you were drunk—and I still can't unsee what I saw that night." He smirked, trying to lighten the mood.

"No, man. I'm serious." Ronin focused, thinking of the suit. In his head, Roland's voice cut in: *Are you sure* this *is a good idea?*

The armor began forming, crawling quickly across his body.

Tommy jerked back against the door. "What the fuck, dude!"

Ronin had the helmet retract, revealing his face. "Listen—it's a long story. Right now, I don't have time to explain. But since you're my best friend, you needed to know before we go into this. Marcus… we're pretty sure he has the same kind of power."

Tommy blinked. "We?"

Ronin smirked. "Another long story. I just need to know if you've still got my back."

Tommy eased a little, nodding. "You know I always have your back. I've had it since you were a kid."

In the rear-view mirror, Ronin caught the flare of police lights—red and blue reflections slicing through the rain. The sirens grew louder, closing in fast.

"Stay back," Ronin muttered. "I don't know how dangerous Marcus is—especially if he has the same kind of pendant as me."

Tommy just shook his head, jaw tight.

Ronin turned into the lot, slamming the brakes. The Bronco skidded, gravel and dust spraying as it drifted to a stop.

22

The shop sprawled before them like a graveyard of forgotten machines. Rusted husks leaned against one another, stripped bare, frames tangled in weeds that had claimed the cracked pavement. A shattered windshield caught the glow of a dying streetlight, fractured like a spiderweb frozen in glass. The air reeked of oil and damp earth, mixed with the far-off hum of highway traffic. Faded gas station signs flickered weakly overhead, bulbs buzzing like ghosts refusing to die.

The awning sagged with age, rattling with each gust of wind. A lone crow perched on a stripped-down chassis, cocking its head like it was judging the wreckage for something worth salvaging.

Among the wrecks sat the cars stolen from Ronin's shop—the ones taken just before the explosions.

Then the first raindrop hit, fat and deliberate against the Bronco's hood. A second followed, then another, until the entire yard echoed with steady patter. The storm had arrived.

Ronin stepped out into the rain. His voice cut through the storm. "Marcus! Get your ass out here. We end this tonight. You've gone too far. If Amy dies, so do you."

Marcus strolled out cockily, cracking his knuckles, adjusting the rings on his fingers. Five men followed— Gavin and Johnny nearest.

"You want us to take him out, boss?" Gavin asked.

Marcus smirked. "No, Gavin. He's all mine. Well, well, Ro. Didn't know about Amy—but that's just a bonus. A casualty of war, as they say."

He started toward Ronin. The suit began to form, mucus-like vines crawling down his skin. His crew froze, wide-eyed. They all turned and ran.

The vines hardened, becoming sleek black-and-grey armor. Axes formed at his sides, crossed in a low holster.

Ronin stepped forward. His own suit flowed across him, locking tight, his sword forming across his back.

The two men closed the distance—

23

And suddenly, red-and-blue lights flooded the lot. Police cars screeched to a stop, sirens cutting through the storm. Officers poured out, weapons raised, boots planted on wet asphalt.

"On your knees! Hands where we can see them!" Officer Whitney shouted.

Marcus didn't move. His mask, featureless black, reflected the lights, his smirk barely visible beneath.

The first shot cracked. The bullet ripped through the rain—then halted an inch from Marcus's chest. Marcus held his hand up, examining the round. He opened his hand and pushed it back towards the officer. It twisted violently before snapping back in the opposite direction.

The officer screamed as the round tore into his shoulder, sending him spinning to the ground.

"Open fire!" Sergeant Donohue roared.

Gunfire erupted. Bullets ripped through the air—but each one froze mid-flight, caught in the pulsing black of Marcus's gloved hand. A moment later, they shot back with unholy precision.

Officer Duffy dropped, screaming as a round shredded his leg. Another bullet ricocheted through the cruiser, glass spraying.

The lot dissolved into chaos—gunfire, screams, the stench of gunpowder and wet asphalt. Cops scrambled for cover as Marcus stood still, letting his suit do the work.

He didn't flinch. He didn't blink. He only watched.

Ronin had seen cruelty before. He knew the kind of men who would rip the world apart for greed and power.

But Marcus wasn't just cruel. He was calculated.

Mathias laughed maniacally, "You think you can outrun death, fool? He is the silence that waits for you at the end, I am his shadow-closer than your breath, hungrier than your fear. Wherever I walk, he follows, and tonight… we walk to you!

Ronin stepped forward. His sword flowed down his wrist, solidifying with a sharp metallic hiss.

Marcus chuckled, his fingers flexing as the veins of his suit pulsed with dark energy.

The rain hammered the dirt-packed ground, transforming it into a reluctant partner in their duel. Across the fractured pavement of the now deserted shop, Marcus's twin axes gleamed while Ronin's single sword shimmered coldly in the sporadic streetlight. Both men circled each other warily, the sound of their footsteps lost beneath the drumming rain.

The initial exchange was explosive. Marcus lunged with a sudden burst of ferocity, one axe slicing downward while the other arced in a deceptive gambit. Alien metal met alien metal with a resounding clash that echoed off the empty vehicles. Ronin deflected the first blow with a practiced parry, but the second attack nicked the air so close that sparks erupted from the impact. In that split second, the world narrowed. Momentum shifted like a double-edged blade. With every slash, Marcus advanced relentlessly. He weaved and twisted, moving as Mathias urged him on.

Mathias had joined Marcus in spirit—they were fighting as one, as were Roland and Ronin.

Ronin, disciplined and methodical, countered each furious assault with precise blocks and replies. A misstep on the wet ground forced Ronin to reel, mud and water momentarily obscuring his vision. But even as vulnerability flashed across his face, he recovered, his eyes steeled with resolve, ready to exploit any hesitation. The gap in Ronin's armor was brief but costly. In one desperate moment,

Marcus spun, his twin weapons slicing through the heavy air in a circular barrage. Ronin slid low, narrowly evading the lethal arc, his blade tracing a protective path in the shifting light. The intense sound of clanging alien steel mingled with the whisper of rain, an eerie symphony celebrating both their defiance and their skill.

The battle loomed larger than the clashing weapons. They propelled themselves around shattered cars and between slivers of light leaking through the broken glass of the wrecks. Each step was a gamble on treacherous, mud-laden ground. Each gasp, a testimony to the pain and perseverance stitched into every blow. Marcus's wild advance was punctuated by fleeting moments of calculated restraint—a misdirected thrust here, a deceptive retreat there—while Ronin countered with relentless, almost balletic precision. As strokes turned into grueling exchanges, the courtyard began to bear the scars of their titanic struggle: shattered cars, muddied tracks, and a lingering scent of iron and rain.

Emotion and fatigue intermingled amid the storm. For a fleeting pause, both men retreated a pace, their chests heaving, eyes locked in mutual hatred. The silence between them was palpable, a suspended breath in a tempest, before the storm of action resumed with even greater intensity. With a guttural cry, Marcus surged forward again, his weapons now a deadly blur. He exploited every gap in the sword's arc, every hesitation in the metal's deflection, driving Ronin into a corner of explosive momentum. Then came the breakthrough—or the brink of despair. At the height of the frenzied clash, as rain mixed with sweat and a solitary cry tore through the night, Marcus's left arm faltered. In that fragile heartbeat, Ronin and Roland recognized their chance. Before Mathias could force Marcus to move, Ronin's blade arced forward, a swift, controlled thrust aimed at the man's chest. Time itself seemed to slow—drops of rain framed as streams of destiny, the shared determination of two warriors written into the very air.

Steel met flesh once more, and a sickening thud punctuated the endless rhythm of clashing weapons. Marcus staggered, his wild maneuvers giving way to controlled desperation and the fierce urge to fight on. Yet every swing, every block, had already told a story—their story from 600 AD until now.

In the final, lingering moments of the duel, the rain softened its fury. Both combatants paused amid the ruins of their battleground, soaked and spent, their weapons hanging heavy with the burdens of battle. Mathias spun, both weapons whirling in tandem, carving an arc through the storm and heavy air. But Ronin recovered, using the momentum to turn his weakness into an advantage. He ducked, narrowly avoiding the flashing steel—and as he rose, his sword struck fast, true, and fatally. A blade deep between the ribs. A gasp. And then, silence.

Roland felt a surge of déjà vu. He had seen this happen before—in his own death. Roland took control of Ronin's body, pulling the sword free just as Marcus used the last of his energy to swing his twin axes up toward Ronin's throat. Roland defended the final attack, knocking the axes from the dying man's hands. They flew across the lot and dissolved to nothing when they finally hit the ground. Roland pushed the sword through Marcus' heart, making sure he was dead this time. As he pulled the blade back, it crept into his arm and reappeared on his back.

A crowd had gathered, all with their phones out, recording the entire fight. Ronin took control of his body again and quickly disappeared into the heap of cars, slipping back into the woods. Tommy jumped in the Bronco and sped off, picking Ronin up around the block. New cops, EMTs, and the fire department screamed toward the scene, blotting out every other sound.

24

The beeping monitors kept the hospital room quiet and steady, but inside Ronin's mind, there was another voice. Roland's. "You did well." He barely moved, barely acknowledged it, but Roland was always there—a whisper just behind his thoughts, a tether to something ancient, something far beyond the explosion that had nearly killed Amy.

Across the room, Amy lay still, her burns wrapped tightly. She had learned about him on the television, watching footage of a man moving through chaos with impossible speed. Tommy sat beside him, tossing a paper cup between his hands.

"You realize you're officially a superhero now, right?"

Ronin replied, "This stays with us, and I'm no superhero." He exhaled sharply, his fingers pressing against his temple. "I don't even know what I am."

Roland's voice hummed with approval and understanding. "You are one of us. A knight and warrior of our lineage."

Amy shifted slightly, wincing before her tired gaze found him.

"You could've told me."

"I barely understand it myself," Ronin admitted.

She was quiet for a moment, then sighed. "So… what happens now?"

Ronin closed his eyes briefly, listening—not just to his own thoughts, but to the one that had been with him since the moment this all began.

"You are not alone. I will always be here when you need me."

He opened his eyes again, looking at Amy, at Tommy, at the flickering television screen that replayed his actions over and over.

"…Now?" He let out a long-held breath, leaning back against the chair. "Now we figure it out. Together."

And somewhere in the depths of his mind, Roland approved.

PART FOUR
MEGENDRA'S LAST STAND

1

Megendra and Seoul had been bound to Roland and Mathias, their fates intertwined even beyond death. It was Seoul who had sealed them with the closing spell after they fell, ensuring their spirits would never escape. Yet Megendra had eluded capture, and as the spell was cast, he secretly embedded his own key within it—a hidden weakness that would one day unravel the enchantment.

During the climactic battle between Ronin and Marcus, Megendra took his final gamble. As Marcus fought fiercely, unaware of the lurking spirit, Megendra forced his essence into the pendant hanging from the warrior's neck. The decisive strike that felled Marcus sent the necklace hurtling through the air, crashing onto the bloodied earth. In the chaos that followed, neither the officers nor the relentless swarm of reporters noticed the small, seemingly insignificant trinket. The battlefield was searched, cleared, and forgotten—but the pendant remained.

2

Days later, a young Asian man named Han was rushing to a job interview when his gaze landed on the discarded necklace. He paused, bending down to examine it.

Han had been a troublemaker since childhood—restless, reckless, and defiant from the age of five. Abandoned on an orphanage's doorstep at only three days old, he bounced through foster homes, each one unwilling or unable to tame his wild nature. By twenty-three, he had aged out of the system, left with nowhere to go and no one to turn to. The generosity of friends had worn thin, leaving him stranded, forced to scrape by however he could.

Han was tall for an Asian man, standing at an imposing 6'2". His frame was sculpted by years of relentless workouts and jiu-jitsu classes—first as a necessity to fend off bullies in high school, later a complement to his combative attitude. His long, black, braided hair was always neatly done, his sharp brown eyes full of a dangerous charm he often wielded to manipulate and exploit others. Women fell for his intensity, unaware of his selfish intentions.

Without hesitation, he scooped up the necklace, darted his eyes around to ensure no one was watching, then shoved it into his pocket. He wasn't interested in sentimentality or mystery, only survival. If the pawnshop gave him enough for it, he might afford one more night at the dingy motel he'd been crashing in. Maybe even get some decent takeout.

Little did Han know, the pendant's secrets were far from dormant.

Han had never wanted to be a dishwasher anyway, so he skipped the interview. Finding the necklace felt like a sign, an excuse not to show up. He turned away from his intended path, walking a few blocks toward the pawn shop instead.

Stepping inside, he let his gaze wander over the cluttered shelves of forgotten valuables. His eyes landed on an antique mirror, its ornate frame worn with time. Never one to pass up a chance to admire himself, Han struck a casual pose in front of it. But as he adjusted his stance, his stomach tightened. A shadowy figure loomed behind him in the reflection. His pulse jumped.

He spun around—but the shop was empty. When he turned back to the mirror, the figure had vanished. He exhaled sharply, shaking his head. Fatigue. That had to be it.

Pushing the unease aside, he walked up to the counter, offering a nod to Jason, the burly shop owner who had dealt with him plenty of times before.

"Welcome back, valued customer," Jason boomed, his laughter deep and familiar. "What do you have for me today? And for the love of God, please tell me it's not stolen like your last haul. The cops were breathing down my neck for weeks, trying to figure out where that mess came from."

Han let out a forced chuckle, slipping the pendant and necklace onto the counter. The chain was a simple herringbone style, but the pendant was striking—a serpent coiled in an elegant twist, ruby eyes glinting under the shop's dim lighting.

"I promise it's not stolen," Han said smoothly. "I found it at the crime scene where those freaks with superpowers had their little showdown. What can I get for it?"

Jason narrowed his eyes, picking up the necklace and running the chain through his fingers. Then, with a practiced motion, he grabbed his jeweler's loupe and examined the pendant closely.

"You sure this isn't stolen?" he muttered, shifting the pendant under the light. "Because this thing is high quality."

Han grinned. Good quality meant good money.

"Nah, man, it was right there by the curb. No idea how nobody else saw it. Guess it's my lucky day," he said casually.

Jason studied the necklace with growing interest.

"Alright, it's high quality, and it's unique… I'll offer you $1,000."

Han let out a sharp laugh. "Come on, you know it's worth twice that."

Jason flashed his signature grin, his gold tooth catching the dim fluorescent light.

"Maybe, but this is a pawn shop. I have to store it, clean it, display it… etc., etc., etc." He stretched the words out deliberately. "But since you're such a good friend and such a loyal customer, I'll be generous and offer you $1,300."

Han grimaced. "$1,600."

Jason narrowed his eyes, weighing it over.

"$1,500—final offer. Take it or leave it."

Han didn't hesitate, extending his hand. "Cash."

Jason shook his head. "I'll be right back; I don't keep that much cash up here. And if I find out this thing's stolen, I'm giving the cops your name this time," he warned, disappearing through the tacky hanging beads toward the safe.

Left alone, Han turned back to the antique mirror. That vision—whatever he'd seen—still lingered in his mind. He stared into the glass, searching for any trace of the shadowy figure, but all he found was a faint shimmer, barely perceptible. Probably just old glass, he reasoned. That's why it ended up in a pawn shop. Then, in the back of his mind, so faint it was almost a breath, came a voice. A whisper. Han didn't know it yet, but this was the moment everything began to go wrong.

Jason reappeared, meticulously counting the money before sliding each bill into Han's hand. Han snatched the cash greedily, mumbling a half-hearted "thanks" as he stuffed it into his pocket. Without another word, he turned on his heel and trudged back to his run-down motel. There, he paid for another month's stay, pocketing the remainder before heading out again. That night, Han ended up at the China Moon restaurant. He ordered an impressive feast—Crab Rangoon, General Tso's Chicken, white rice, Lo Mein, sweet and sour pork—alongside three bottles of Mountain Dew and two bottles of rice wine. It had been ages since he'd indulged in a proper meal or even a decent drink. When the food arrived at the counter, he carried it back to his motel room and devoured nearly everything. Unable to resist, he mixed the soda with the wine, a crude cocktail that left him passed out on the scratchy motel bed.

3

The next morning, Han awoke to a dull throb in his skull. Shuffling to the bathroom, he splashed cold water on his face—and froze. In the mirror, hanging around his neck, was the necklace with its pendant.

"What the fuck, where did this come from?" he muttered, panic tightening in his chest. "Fuck, I hope I didn't rob Jason's place in some drunken stupor."

He tugged at the chain, but it wouldn't budge. Searching for a clasp that wasn't there, he growled in frustration. "Ugh, what the fuck?" Finally, he threw up his hands and stepped into the shower.

Under the steady spray and fogged glass, he thought he saw a figure. A face, familiar, lingering in the mist. He yanked the curtain aside—nothing. His heart hammered as he tried to steady himself. Just the alcohol, he told himself. All the alcohol from last night.

After dressing, he checked his phone, bracing for an angry message from Jason if the necklace had been stolen. But there was nothing—no calls, no texts. In that eerie quiet, the unease only grew.

With some money left, Han budgeted carefully: another few weeks at the motel, food, and a few new clothes. He even managed to wash the ones he had. After that binge at China Moon, he decided to eat sparingly. No alcohol either. The brutal hangover had nearly convinced him he was losing his mind.

That evening, he kept it simple—pizza and a Breaking Bad marathon. At some point, exhaustion dragged him under.

4

Han woke with a jolt—but not in his motel room.

He was somewhere else. A cavern stretched around him, dimly lit by a flickering fire pit. Above it, a large cauldron hung precariously from a crude frame. Makeshift tables ringed the flames, cluttered with vials, dark potions, and ancient tools. Damp stone walls glistened with mildew; the air reeked of earth and decay.

Han's voice cracked in the silence. "What the fuck… this is one wicked dream."

Movement answered him. A hooded figure emerged from the shadows, slow, deliberate, stepping into the firelight. His voice was gravelly, low, unsettling.

"This is no dream, boy. You and I are connected."

As the man drew closer, his features came into view— and Han's stomach dropped.

It was him. The man from the mirror. From the shower fog.

Han's pulse hammered against his ribs, echoing in the cavern's stillness. This wasn't a dream. It was worse. A living nightmare.

Paralyzed, he watched as the hooded figure studied him with cruel amusement. Megendra could see the fear in Han's face, and it pleased him. He needed this boy, needed the power he could take from him. Possession was one option. But control—manipulation—would be far easier.

"I've seen the pain in your mind—the anger, the judgment, the hunger for power," the mage said, his voice a sickly blend of false compassion and persuasion. "I can give that to you, now that we are connected."

Han squared his shoulders, forcing defiance into his voice. "How the hell are we connected? How did you even get me here?" But beneath his words, uncertainty lingered.

Megendra stepped closer, gliding more than walking. "Our destinies brought us together. When you picked up the necklace, you invited me in. I am now a part of you."

Han's fists clenched. "That's bullshit."

Megendra only smiled, extending his arms in a dramatic flourish as he gestured to the cavern surrounding them. "As for how I got you here? This… is your mind. But I control the scenery."

With a flick of his staff, the damp cavern dissolved, reshaping into the dingy motel room where Han had last been. Another wave of his hand, and suddenly they stood in the pawn shop, another wave, and they were in the exact place where Han had found the necklace—where his fate had unknowingly been sealed. One final motion, and the world shifted again.

Now they stood in a sprawling mansion perched on a hill, overlooking a glittering waterfront. Sunlight streamed through floor-to-ceiling windows, casting golden hues across marble floors and pristine leather furnishings. Outside, parked in the driveway, gleamed a bright blue 1968 AMX with the Go-Package. Han's dream car.

Megendra watched with dark amusement as Han took it all in, eyes wide with awe. The hook was set.

"This one speaks to you," Megendra murmured.

Han swallowed hard. It did. Everything about this place—the wealth, the beauty, the impossible promise—was intoxicating.

Megendra leaned in, his voice dripping with sinister satisfaction. "All this could be yours. Power. Wealth. Revenge on those who judged you, who discarded you like garbage. They could all be put in their place."

Han didn't move, didn't speak, but Megendra saw it—the boy was wavering.

Finally, Han broke the silence, his voice cautious but undeniably intrigued. "What do I need to do?"

Megendra's words slid into his thoughts like silk. "I need to be resurrected. With modern science and technology combined with my ancient magic, it can be done. But I require three relics, ones I cannot retrieve in this ghostly form. I need your body to collect them." His tone deepened, heavy with promise. "Once I return, you will have all the wealth and power you deserve, earned through the suffering this world has thrown at you."

Han stood still, weighing the words, but Megendra could already see the decision forming. His will was fragile, his anger sharp, his hunger for control just strong enough to bend him.

"Fine," Han said at last. "Where do we start?"

Megendra smiled, sifting through Han's mind, extracting memories until he found what he needed. "The small island of Molokai holds the first piece of the crown. I discovered all three fragments long before I had to leave my kingdom. I remember everything."

Han narrowed his eyes. "What crown?"

With a flick of his hand, the air rippled like painted light on a canvas. Megendra's voice grew deeper as the vision unfolded before them.

"The Crown of Severed Dominion. Long ago, King Irithar the Undying sought to defy mortality. He forged the crown from cursed metals and wove soul-binding magic into its core. It granted him eternal reign—his body would never age, his soul would persist even when his flesh was destroyed."

But Megendra held back the darker truth. The crown's immortality was fueled by the spirits of Irithar's subjects, their life force siphoned away to sustain him.

"When Irithar's cruelty grew unbearable, three rebels rose against him: the Fatesworn Sorcerer, the Blade-Saint, and the Ashen Monk. Each wielded relics and weapons capable of severing his unnatural existence. In the final battle, they shattered the crown in three blows.

The Wraithspike snapped when the Blade-Saint pierced Irithar's heart, breaking the soul-binding enchantment.

The Pale Circlet split when the Fatesworn Sorcerer cast his unraveling spell.

The Blackthorn Crest was torn away when the Ashen Monk uttered a forbidden chant, trapping Irithar's essence in the fractured shards."

"Despite their victory," Megendra continued, "Irithar's soul did not perish. It remained bound within the crown's pieces, waiting to be reforged."

Han frowned. "Wouldn't his soul take over once the pieces are put back together?"

Megendra's gaze didn't waver. "His soul is bound, yes. But my magic will purge him. I will strip his presence from every fragment we gather."

Han wasn't convinced, but he didn't push. "Second question—how do you expect us to get to Hawaii? I'm not rich. I barely have enough to eat."

Megendra raised his hand, and the necklace pulsed, alive at last.

The suit answered. It rose like liquid shadow, a ripple across velvet-like fabric that spread and slithered over Han's skin, merging seamlessly with his body. It didn't just clothe him. It claimed him.

The braided strands came alive, twisting across his shoulders and spine, pulsing faintly as though whispering their acceptance. With each movement, the armor sank deeper into him, an extension of his being—his strength, his rage, his weakness.

A long, hooded robe draped over his shoulders. A sleek black mask settled over his face.

Han stared at his reflection, feeling powerful in a way he never had before.

Megendra's voice cut through the moment. "I think you'll find a few places with money ripe for the taking," he said, dark amusement dripping from his words. "Affording us a way to Molokai should be no problem."

5

Han woke in his motel room, momentarily convinced the entire encounter had been a fever dream. But then the voice returned, silken and invasive, curling through his thoughts.

Time to get started.

Over the next few nights, Han moved through the city under the cover of darkness. The suit adapted to every obstacle, molding itself to his will, amplifying his strength until it felt effortless.

The pawn shop was easiest. His sleeve morphed into a crowbar, and with a single pull, he tore the safe door clean off. Seven thousand dollars, just like that. He felt no guilt.

The late-night convenience stores were smaller hauls, but each one added to his growing stash. Every dollar brought him closer to Molokai.

Then came the arts center, where the affluent gathered, draped in wealth, oblivious to the predator in their midst. Han struck fast. Three victims—robbed clean. The men he injured, not out of necessity, but for the thrill. His suit concealed him entirely, erasing his identity, leaving only the rush of power behind.

By the time he returned to his motel, his funds had swelled to twelve thousand. Enough. He pulled up his phone and booked plane tickets and a boat ride. Sitting on the edge of his bed, he murmured to Megendra, informing him of their booked flight to Hawaii and the boat they'd need to reach Molokai.

Megendra approved, his presence retreating into the depths of Han's consciousness. But Han could still feel him there—waiting, watching.

The hunt was only just beginning.

6

The waves whispered before the world did.

Ronin slept uneasily, his body stiff against the unyielding mattress, exhaustion heavy in his bones. The news had given him no comfort, its endless cycle of violence gnawing at the edges of his thoughts. His shop was being rebuilt, his hands kept busy with work, but his mind—his mind was not his own.

It began as ripples in the dark, faint disturbances threading through his consciousness like echoes of something vast and ancient. Then came the images. A man.

Unfamiliar, yet unmistakable. The same thief from the news.

The vision shifted. A burial site, half-swallowed by volcanic stone, the earth itself trying to bury its secrets. Ancient carvings, battered by time, still pulsed with a whisper of power. The air shimmered unnaturally, like heat rising from stone, distorting reality itself. Then the ocean—endless blue crashing against jagged cliffs. A place of reverence. Sacred ground where the footprints of forgotten kings had long since faded.

And at the edge of the world—Han.

Ronin somehow knew his name.

Han stood motionless, his form stretched between realms. The wind did not stir him. Shadows bent toward him, compelled by something unseen.

Then a voice cut through the dream like a blade through mist: *"The first piece lies beneath fire and tide."*

Megendra.

Ronin stiffened. Roland, also present in the dream, recognized the wizard's voice instantly. Han, however, did not react. He only stared ahead, toward the place that called him. Hawaii. Molokai.

Ronin jolted awake with a sharp inhale, the vision seared into the back of his mind. His pulse hammered, each beat a confirmation—this was no dream. The world itself had spoken.

Later that day, Ronin told Tommy and Amy about his dream, his vision. They both agreed that they needed to follow up on it, and Amy figured if it was nothing, they could stay in Hawaii on a vacation that was well deserved.

Han was going west. To the relic buried beneath fire and tide.

The chase had begun.

Ronin grabbed his phone, scrolling fast, searching flights to Molokai.

"Fuck. No flights in." He cursed under his breath, kept scrolling, until finally he found a package: a flight to Hawaii, then a chartered boat to Molokai. It would have to do.

Without hesitation, he booked tickets for all three. Amy could stay behind at the hotel, unwind, while he and Tommy hunted whatever it was they were chasing.

If it was just a dream, fine—they could use a break. But deep down, he knew better. And Roland, ever the voice of unwelcome confirmation, made sure he didn't forget it.

There was no time for doubt. He needed to make sure they were ready to go.

The chase had already begun.

7

Just a few miles away, Han slept, unaware of the silent machinations turning in his mind. Hidden deep, Megendra schemed, his focus locked on the Wraithspike—the first fragment of the crown. Calculations were complete, spells prepared. He would need to extract Irithar's lingering essence from the relic once it was in their grasp.

Five hours remained before Han awoke. Nine before departure. Twelve until they reached Honolulu—a fragment of what had once been Atheria, before the world fractured centuries ago. For now, the mage would rest, dormant, until needed again.

Han arrived at the airport an hour before departure. Noon. He had packed light—just a few clothes, a handful of necessities. Nashville's TSA was effortless, and soon he was boarding his first plane to Los Angeles. After a short layover, he was en route to Honolulu, scheduled to land near midnight.

His plans were already in motion. A boat to Molokai was booked. From there, he and Megendra would search for the Wraithspike.

Later that night, Ronin, Amy, and Tommy boarded their own flight—Seattle first, then a layover, then six grueling hours to Honolulu. A long journey, and each of them prayed for sleep. If not, the time shift would hit even harder the next day.

8

Midnight came, and Han touched down in Honolulu. With stolen cash, he secured a hotel room, bought food, and collapsed into bed. The boat ride was early, and exhaustion weighed heavily.

Dawn arrived, and Han woke sharper than expected. He made his way to Hollo Hollo Charters, where he boarded a boat bound for Molokai. The plan was simple—blend in until they arrived, then slip away unseen.

Megendra's voice surfaced as the boat cut through the waves.

"The cavern lies at the island's edge. Its entrance is submerged, but beyond the threshold, a great chamber awaits the Wraithspike."

Han listened silently.

"There is a guardian," Megendra warned, his tone colder now. "I do not know *its* form. But your armor will suffice. And if not—I will intervene."

Han's face twisted, drawing odd glances from nearby passengers.

"The fuck do you mean, *guardian*? You told me I was stealing relics, not fighting for them!" he whispered.

The mage snapped, his presence within Han's mind lashing out — a phantom strike, like being slapped inside his own skull.

"Hush, boy!" Megendra's voice cut through him. "You will take the Wraithspike. You seek power, wealth? Then act like a man. Do what must be done!"

Han instinctively flinched, earning yet another wary glance from the tourists.

Upon arrival, he wasted no time slipping away unnoticed. Dense foliage swallowed him whole as he trekked inland. The thick forest gave way to a mile-wide guava field, followed by towering kiawe, koa, and lama trees.

Three miles later, he reached the island's outermost tip, gazing over the endless Pacific.

That was when he felt it — a vibration, subtle yet undeniable, humming through his bones. The relic was close. Without hesitation, he stepped into the ocean.

The deeper he dove, the stronger the vibrations became, like a pulse threading through the water itself. Then, nestled within submerged rock, he found it: the entrance.

He surfaced in a cavern beneath the island, vast and silent. The air was thick with the scent of decay and embers.

At the center rested the Wraithspike, its jagged, spectral form pulsing with an eerie white glow. It called to him —

not in words, but in sensation, a promise of power threaded through his bones.

Then, movement. The ground stirred beneath the relic. Slowly, a figure rose. Charred ceremonial robes clung to its shifting form, its presence flickering like a broken signal, glitching through space as if reality itself struggled to define it. Its mask was fractured, its eye sockets hollow. A single ember flickered faintly within.

It spoke, its voice splintered into many, weaving together in a discordant chorus.

"You seek the Wraithspike. You shall join the rest of the forgotten."

Han exhaled, smirking beneath his armor. "They always say something like that."

The Husk lunged. Han's armor responded instantly, his sleeve morphing into a blade as he met the strike. Steel clashed. Sparks erupted. He twisted, shifting his weapon mid-strike into a serrated edge. The guardian staggered, its mask splintering further. But something was wrong. It wasn't weakening.

Han stepped back, watching as the Husk grew sharper, faster, more dangerous. Each strike only fed it, clarifying its form. He scowled. "Fine." Brute force wouldn't work. He'd overwhelm it instead.

His armor rippled, shifting into twin axes as he launched forward.

The Husk mirrored him, its weapon morphing into a grotesque imitation of Han's own.

"Fuck, it's learning." Han yelled.

Then Megendra's voice slithered into Han's mind.

"Enough. You cannot slay the Husk. You must take it. Bind it. Consume it."

Han hesitated only for a breath. Then, with deliberate intent, he extended his hand. The armor obeyed. Tendrils of liquid-dark metal lashed forward, seizing the Husk's shifting form.

The guardian screamed — not in rage, but in recognition. It knew. It struggled, but Han did not falter. His armor swallowed it, dragging its fractured essence into the folds of shifting flesh.

A weight settled inside Han's mind. Faces flashed before him — those who had come before, those who had failed. Then, silence.

The chamber stilled. The Wraithspike clattered to the ground, spinning once before settling.

Han stepped forward and wrapped his fingers around the relic. Power surged through him — colder, sharper than before. Within his armor, he felt the Husk's presence lingering, watching, waiting. Then, it was gone.

Megendra's laughter echoed in his thoughts.

"Good. Now onward."

9

By the time Ronin and his team landed in Honolulu, Han was already en route to the cavern, his mission underway.

The trio checked into their hotel, weighed down by fatigue and the tension of unseen threats. Rest was necessary; there was no saving the world without a clear mind.

Ronin collapsed onto the bed, falling into a deep sleep almost immediately. But sleep brought no peace — only visions.

He saw where Han and Megendra had gone.

He saw the cave, black as obsidian, humming with an ancient menace.

He saw the clash — Han versus the Husk — the echo of steel, the ripple of dark armor, predator within predator.

Before the battle concluded, Ronin jolted awake, breath ragged. They'd only been asleep for about four hours.

In his mind, Roland was already speaking: "You know what you have to do. Go to the cavern. See what happened. See if they obtained the Wraithspike."

Ronin roused Tommy and informed Amy.

"We're heading out."

She nodded groggily, understanding without question.

Ronin and Tommy made their way to the pier, joining the queue as the boat approached the dock. Their departure was set for noon.

"What exactly are we looking for?" Tommy asked, adjusting his pack.

"I'm not sure," Ronin admitted, voice heavy with frustration. "Han made it to the cavern. I saw the fight. But the dream ended before I knew how it played out."

As they climbed the boarding ramp, a man brushed past Ronin. Just a slight touch—but it was enough.

A vision pierced his mind. Han again. Mid-battle. The same flickering shadows, the same morphing armor. Then it vanished, leaving Ronin breathless.

Tommy noticed. "You good? Not to be *punny*, but you look like the wind just got knocked out of your sails."

Ronin steadied himself, eyes narrowing as he pointed subtly toward the man who had bumped him. "That was Han."

Tommy's expression twisted. "Holy shit, are you serious?" He glanced around, but it was too late—boarding was already underway.

"Damn. Can't exactly jump ship now."

"No," Ronin said grimly. "But if he's walking free, it means he won. We need to get to that cave and find out what we're dealing with."

They took their seats, tension knotting between them. As the boat pulled away from the dock, the horizon stretched open, the blue Pacific whispering secrets they were only beginning to understand.

Han felt it too—the presence, familiar, unwanted.

Megendra sensed Roland's presence as well. The realization struck them both, and they hastened their pace, weaving through the crowd before vanishing onto the island.

10

Once inside his room, Han packed quickly. In his mind, he addressed the mage.

"Where next? Where's the Pale Circlet?"

Megendra was silent at first, sifting through Han's fragmented geography, pulling from memories buried deep.

"Socotra Island. Yemen."

Han pulled out his laptop, searching. He read aloud: "Socotra Island—known for its alien-like landscapes. Flights are limited, typically arranged through local travel agencies. You'll need a charter flight, usually from Abu Dhabi, with the assistance of a licensed Socotra tour operator."

He muttered under his breath, scrolling until he found the nearest travel agency. The island was full of them. The closest one had an opening in an hour. Han booked it without hesitation.

11

Ronin and Tommy moved with the same urgency, slipping away from the tour unseen.

Ronin followed the path burned into his memory, the cavern from his vision pulling him forward. As they neared the water's edge, Ronin clenched his fists—and in response, his suit awakened, encasing him in fluid darkness.

Tommy still marveled at it. A tendril rippled from Ronin's back, forming into a sleek diver's mask.

Tommy eyed it, then looked at Ronin. "What the hell am I supposed to do with that?"

Ronin cocked his head. No words needed.

Tommy sighed, grabbing the mask. "Fine." He secured it and followed Ronin into the water.

The ocean swallowed them. Depths stretched endlessly, but Ronin relied on the vision—its details precise, its guidance absolute.

And then, there it was. The entrance.

They surfaced inside the cavern, stepping onto slick stone as Ronin's suit slithered back into its pendant.

The air was thick with echoes of battle. Scars marred the walls—evidence of violence, of power unleashed. What had once been a sacred resting place now bore the weight of destruction.

Tommy moved first, tracing the edges of fractured stone, absorbing the beauty that had once lived in this hidden sanctuary. Then he found it.

The place where the Wraithspike had rested.

He studied the remnants closely, curiosity turning to reverence. His hand lifted, fingers reaching to touch—

"NO!" Roland's voice ripped through Ronin's thoughts.

But it was too late.

Electricity exploded through Tommy's body, spiraling in violent shades of blue, purple, and white. Light spun in chaotic torrents, weaving in and out of him, through him. His hair stood on end. His eyes went white.

Silence.

Ronin's suit reacted, armor unfolding, wrapping around him instinctively. He lunged, grabbing Tommy, pulling hard, desperate. But the stone pulsed again and—BOOM.

They were thrown backward, crashing into a waist-deep pool. Tommy lay still. His eyes remained white.

Roland's voice pounded in Ronin's skull. No pulse. Panic gripped him. Lightning still buzzed across the stone Tommy had touched.

Ronin had an idea. A reckless one.

"Roland, I need help. This could kill both of us. If something goes wrong, pull me away."

Roland read his thoughts and agreed without hesitation. Ronin peeled back the armor on his hands.

Dragging Tommy closer, he positioned them both near the stone's resting place. One bare hand pressed against Tommy's chest. The other reached toward the electrified rock.

The armor peeled back from his pointer fingers.

Contact.

Heat seared through Ronin, blistering agony tearing through his veins. His free hand peeled away from its armor too, palm pressing to Tommy's chest.

Tommy's body arched violently as the electrical shock tried to jumpstart his heart; his body lifted off the ground. Roland commanded the suit, shielding Ronin's hand, dampening the pain, forcing the pulse into Tommy's body.

Silence. Nothing.

Ronin gritted his teeth. "Come on, Tommy. You're not going out like this."

He repeated the process, shocking Tommy's chest again. Nothing.

Tears burned in Ronin's eyes. "Tommy, fuck, don't die on me!"

Desperation consumed him. Ronin ripped the armor back from his entire forearm, exposing himself fully. He grabbed Tommy, pulling him against his chest—one hand over his heart, the other fully on the stone itself.

Pain erupted. Every nerve screamed. Fire beneath his skin. Lightning, threading through his muscles. His mind shattering under the pressure. His body breaking, his head splitting apart.

And then—LIGHT.

Roland acted fast, forcing the suit to cover Ronin's grip again. Then, Tommy gasped. His eyes snapped open—color flooding back—only to erupt with a mist of lightning.

He screamed, incoherent words spilling out, his voice fractured, not entirely his own. Then, lower, steadier—his voice finally broke through.

"I know where he's going next."

"Holy shit, Tommy, you're alive," Ronin gasped, drained and shaking.

Tommy sat up slowly, blinking away the static haze still buzzing through his vision. "I know where he's going next," he muttered, voice trembling. "And I don't know what happened, but I feel… wrong. Like something is inside me. Like I've been invaded. Body-snatcher type shit."

He turned toward Ronin—and froze.

Horror spread across his face as he scrambled backward. "What the fuck is going on, Ronin?"

Ronin scanned the cavern. "What? What do you see?"

His suit rippled back over him out of instinct, all but the headpiece. Tommy's eyes widened, locked on something Ronin couldn't see.

"Who's that standing behind you?"

Ronin spun around. Nothing.

Tommy's voice shook. "Is that… Roland?"

Roland's voice echoed in Ronin's mind—and this time aloud. Tommy heard it too.

"He can see me," Roland said, stunned.

Ronin turned again—and saw it. The ghostly figure of Roland materialized beside him, spectral yet steady.

"How the hell is this possible?" Ronin murmured.

Before an answer could form, fog began to coil across the stone floor. Smoke wound through the cavern like incense, rising until a new figure appeared—silvery, still.

A spirit. A warrior. The Blade-Saint.

He stood at the eye of the storm—calm, poised, radiating ancient gravity. His armor bore no sigils of conquest, only litanies of grief and grace. Every scratch, a sermon. Every dent, a memory. Above his head hovered a fractured halo of steel—magnetized by oath, not divinity. His eyes glowed dimly, like incense burning at a funeral altar: calm, mournful, but lit with judgment.

His blade, *Saintthorn*, was not forged for war but for truth. Born from the spine of a martyr, cooled in sacred oil— it did not sing often. But when it did, the air itself wept.

"I am Thalen Vire," he said, voice resonant and sorrowful. "The Blade-Saint. I have seen in this man's mind that you pursue those called Megendra and Han. A monster now wears the face of a mortal. He has defeated my guardian and I—we were bound to the Wraithspike.”

The three stood in stunned silence: Ronin, Tommy, and even Roland’s ghost.

Finally, Roland spoke. “We are pursuing them. They stole the relic. We need to understand what they’re planning. And we need your help.”

Thalen’s gaze swept the ruined cavern, now glowing faintly with ghost light. “You cannot defeat him alone,” he warned. “The Wraithspike is one of three shards of the Crown of Severed Dominion.”

Then he recited its tale—the same one Megendra had whispered to Han.

“I do not yet know their intentions,” Thalen continued, “but there is only one reason to gather the fragments: to re-forge the crown and build a vessel that cannot die—for the evil mage.”

The words struck like thunder.

“I have bestowed my power upon this mortal,” Thalen said, gesturing to Tommy. “His heart is just. His cause is worthy. He carries the truth of where the Pale Circlet and the Blackthorn Crest lie hidden.”

Tommy rose slowly, breathing shallow, mind reeling as visions and emotions flooded in—not learned, but remembered. In an instant, he became something else.

Power coursed through him like memory. Images flashed—men of faith turned warriors, miracles born from grief. His powers revealed themselves, ancient and terrible:

His relic blade, *Saintthorn,* now formed across his back—a weapon that resonated with sin. The more guilt it sensed in an opponent, the heavier and brighter it became, blazing with divine wrath. Against the innocent, it refused to strike.

Tommy's mind fractured and reforged all at once. As he steadied himself, the hum of *Saintthorn* grew, and one truth settled deep within him—

The path ahead would demand everything.

But he was ready.

When he recovered, he stood tall, quiet strength radiating from him. As his hand touched the hilt of *Saintthorn,* a menyoroi mask formed over his face, and a burst of smoke engulfed him.

When it cleared, he was transformed.

His suit was sleek and black, accented with sharp streaks of blue. Plate-like armor shielded his chest and shoulders, giving him a powerful silhouette. Segmented blue bracers reinforced his arms and legs, while a matching belt anchored the design—a vertical blue stripe running down his torso. Hinged joints promised speed and precision. He looked like something forged from shadow and storm.

His eyes glowed faintly, blue and electric.

Thalen was gone, vanished into the smoke that had birthed him. His ghost finally passed on.

Ronin stared, stunned. "Holy hell, Tommy… look at you."

Tommy grinned. The glow dimmed, revealing warm brown beneath. "Christ, I look like a Mortal Kombat character," he said, striking a pose. "*Finish him!*"

Ronin laughed, shaking his head. But the humor faded quickly.

"The next relic's in Yemen," Tommy said, tone tightening. "Han's probably already halfway there. We need to move—fast."

Ronin didn't hesitate. He pulled Tommy into a tight embrace. "Then let's get going."

Tommy nodded, sheathing the sword. In an instant, the suit vanished, the weapon with it. Yet he could still feel it—its weight, its readiness—bonded to him beyond material.

Roland faded silently back into Ronin's mind, and the two men turned toward the light, carrying with them the knowledge that the world might soon hinge on what came next.

12

The morning sun over Honolulu did little to ease the tension pressing behind Han's eyes. The moment he'd booked the appointment, he felt time tightening around him like a noose. Megendra was quiet—too quiet—as if calculating a dozen dark paths in parallel.

Han stepped into the narrow, over-air-conditioned office of Pacific Dream Travel. Pamphlets of smiling couples on white sand beaches fanned out across the counter. Behind it, a tired-looking agent in a lei-print shirt and reading glasses greeted him with a smile that barely reached her eyes.

"Can I help you?" she asked.

"Yeah. I need to get to Socotra. Yemen. Fast."

Her fingers tapped the keyboard, eyes squinting at the monitor. "Flights to Yemen are… rare. And Socotra's even trickier. You usually have to go through Abu Dhabi. We work with a charter company there, but all the seats are full for the next ten days. I'm sorry, sir."

Han clenched his jaw. "There's got to be something—cancellations, private charters, anything."

"Believe me, I've checked."

Inside Han's mind, Megendra stirred. "This one lacks vision," the mage whispered. "Let me come forward."

Han exhaled and stepped aside in his head, pretending to scroll through his phone. A shimmer passed behind his irises—his pupils dilating into pools of starlit void.

Megendra looked through eyes that weren't his. Through the code. His will slipped between the flicker of the air-conditioning vents and the faint hum of electricity.

"Bend the weave," he muttered. "Open the path."

The travel agent blinked. She unknowingly cancelled someone's flight to Yemen. She woke from the trance. Her monitor flashed, glitched, then refreshed. She leaned forward, confused.

"Well… that's odd," she murmured. "A charter seat just opened up. Someone canceled on a private Abu Dhabi connector, and the connecting flight to Socotra's been cleared. I… I didn't see this before."

Han returned as Megendra receded. He masked his grin. "I'll take it."

She typed furiously, processing the ticket. "You leave in six hours. It'll be tight."

"Wouldn't have it any other way," Han replied.

As he stepped outside, the tropical breeze hit his face like a warning. Megendra's voice came again—proud, predatory. "The tides shift in our favor. But beware, our enemies move too."

Han slid on his sunglasses and kept walking. Yemen was calling, and the Pale Circlet wasn't going to wait.

Han settled into the plush leather seat of the chartered Gulfstream, the midday sun blazing over Honolulu's harbor behind him. Through the small oval window, the boat docks shrank to toy-like dots. Megendra's presence drifted through his mind—cool, patient.

"The journey itself will test you," the mage murmured. "Watch closely."

Han nodded. The engines roared to life, and the jet lifted smoothly above the clouds, banking west toward Abu Dhabi.

Inside the cabin, time seemed to warp. Every surface gleamed with polished chrome and midnight-blue leather, lit by soft overhead lamps. Han thumbed through his travel documents, mind elsewhere. Megendra's awareness flickered between him and the horizon—an unspoken reminder that this flight was more than transit.

Halfway across the ocean, the cabin lights dimmed, and the engine's hum deepened. Outside, the sky turned a bruised purple. Han wiped a bead of sweat from his temple, though the air remained cool.

"Are you uncomfortable, sir?" the pilot's voice crackled over the intercom.

Han shook his head. "Just… altitude."

13

Arrival in Abu Dhabi felt like waking from a fever dream. The blazing desert sun hit Han's face as the jet taxied to a secluded terminal. A single, white-robed agent met him on the tarmac —no questions, no words. Within minutes, Han was ushered into a waiting Falcon 900 charter bound for Socotra.

The second flight soared above endless dunes, waves of gold stretching to the horizon. Here, there were no apparitions—only silence, broken by the steady thrust of the engines.

When the wheels finally touched down on Socotra's makeshift runway, Han stepped into a world unlike any other.

A wind swept across the tarmac, carrying a scent of brine, resin, and something ancient.

The shoreline was lined with towering bottle trees, their swollen trunks twisting skyward like petrified giants. Beyond them rose the Dragon's Blood Forest—limbless trees bleeding crimson sap into glassy pools. Further still, the land shattered into limestone "dragon's teeth," boulder forests carved by time and wind, a maze of natural sculpture.

Megendra's voice guided him once more. "The Pale Circlet rests where earth and sky meet."

Han strode across the cracked red earth, each footstep kicking up fine dust that smelled of iron and salt. Shadows lengthened as the sun dipped toward the western sea.

By twilight, Han neared the Qalandiya cliffs—the rumored site of a cave hollowed beneath the earth, lit only by phosphorescent lichens. The mouth gaped like a wound in the rock, half-submerged by the incoming tide.

He anchored his pack, waded in, and the chill water climbed to his thighs. Inside, faint blue luminescence pulsed along the cave walls, leading him deeper until a stone dias emerged from the sand.

Resting atop it lay a delicate circlet of pale gold, its filigree twisting like seagrass. Ghostly runes shimmered across its surface—the promise of immortality, and the curse entwined within.

Megendra's sigh was almost reverent. "The Pale Circlet. One step closer to rebirth."

Han reached forward, ready to steal, to fight, to claim his destiny. But as his fingers brushed the metal, the wind surged behind him.

"You are not alone…"

In the shifting glow of the moss, eyes blinked open in the darkness beyond.

The island had only begun to reveal its secrets.

The Pale Circlet's weight settled in his palm. Megendra's voice pulsed softly through his mind. "You've done well. But now you must master the armor you wear—this fight will be far more dangerous than the last. Its last master left too much to the imagination.”

Alone on the cavern shore, Han closed his eyes and focused. The suit’s panels stirred under his skin, humming with latent power. He willed his forearm plates to part; cobalt-blue vents hissed open, exhaling vapor. Pressure gathered behind him, and with a push of will, the armor launched him forward in a jet-propelled leap. He landed cleanly, sand spraying at his feet.

“Excellent,” Megendra said. “Now, shape the water to your blade.”

Han swept his palm through the humid air. The gauntlet at his wrist rippled, reforming into a serrated hydro-blade of glowing seawater. He tested the weapon with a flick—then sliced a stalagmite cleanly down the middle. The blade collapsed back into liquid, folding into the vents.

“Defend yourself.”

Instinct took over. Han raised his arm, and a domed shield blossomed before him—its surface alive with oceanic motion. Droplets struck and vanished into ripples, absorbed into its living pattern. When he released the thought, the shield dissolved into a faint shimmer clinging to his wrist.

Megendra’s laughter echoed through his head. “Every gesture can shape the tide. You are no longer merely armored—you are the armor.”

Han opened his hand, watching the last traces of light fade. Each discovery bound the suit closer to his will. Under the rising moonlight filtering through the cavern’s mouth, he stood still, every breath attuned to the armor that would carry him into the final struggle.

14

Han entered more confident than ever before. The chamber trembled as Han placed the Pale Circlet atop the stone dias. Megendra's voice cut through his thoughts. "Be ready. This guardian's fury rivals the sea itself."

From the flooded archway, the Coral Warden rose—a colossal shape born of salt and storm. Towering twenty feet high, its body was sculpted from bleached coral and tide-worn limestone. Iridescent shell inlays glowed faintly across its chest, and veins of bioluminescent algae pulsed like liquid fire. From its back sprouted limbs of driftwood, gnarled and knotted like the roots of a drowned tree. Two polished opals, set deep in its granite helm, flared to life. Steam hissed at its feet as it took its first thunderous step.

"You trespass upon this reef's sacred trust," it rumbled, its voice a breaking wave. "Return what belongs to the sea— or be buried beneath it like so many before you."

Megendra's voice echoed in Hans's ears sharply. "Fight, Han. Show it the price of defiance."

Han sprang aside as the Warden's massive fist slammed down, shattering the stone dias into coral fragments. He rolled, suit plates shifting to absorb the shock.

"Use your vents—for your father's sake!" Megendra roared.

Han triggered the vents. Twin jets erupted, propelling him skyward. From above, he brought down two hydro-blades in a cascading strike. The Warden's coral shell

223

cracked; algae veins sputtered. Yet the guardian endured, swinging a driftwood arm in retaliation. Han blurred out of reach, the wooden limb smashing into stone where he'd stood a breath before.

The Warden advanced, algae veins flaring with fury. Han thrust out a palm, and a domed barrier of living water surged to life, scattering coral shards like a tempest. In the same breath, he followed with a counterstrike—sending a concussive wave of compressed water through the barrier and into the Warden's midriff. The veins around its ribs burst open, spilling bioluminescent slurry across the sand.

Megendra stepped forward, taking control. He wove ancient runes through the air, a lattice of sapphire light binding the Warden's wounds open. "It bleeds," he said, "but it fights on."

A hush fell. From the shimmering haze above the remaining dias, violet mist gathered into a tall, robed figure. Embroidered frost-star patterns glimmered across his cloak. This was the Fatesworn Sorcerer—Aleric Vire—robust despite his spectral frailty, staff crowned with a frozen lotus of fallen souls. His pale face was half-hidden beneath a rune-etched hood, and where his eyes should have been, glowed twin shards of glacial light.

With a voice like a chorus of mourning winds, he chanted, "You dare try to sever fate's balance?"

He thrust both hands downward. Bolts of violet-blue lightning leapt from his fingertips, lancing through the Warden's fractured coral. Where Han had wounded it, the algae veins knitted together, flaring brighter than before.

Thorns of living coral regrew in seconds; driftwood branches twisted into new whips. The guardian straightened, renewed, and roared in triumph.

Megendra hissed, "He's fused his soul with the Warden—its wounds heal at will!"

Han staggered back, breath ragged. "We have to break his hold!"

Megendra surged forward again in Hans' body, his hands tracing sigils in the air. A ring of crackling stormlight burst outward, wrapping the Warden's shoulders in chains of blue fire. The guardian howled, algae veins pulsing, driftwood limbs thrashing against the bonds.

"Now, Han!" Megendra commanded, relinquishing control. "Channel the Circlet's grace through your suit!"

Han's chest plates unfolded, revealing a chamber beneath. He pressed the Pale Circlet against it and willed its power into a single beam—pure, searing light—lancing straight into the Warden's merging core.

The Fatesworn shrieked. His mist-form fractured; shards of violet ash drifted away. His voice echoed through the cavern as the bond unraveled. The Warden trembled, its coral shell splitting anew.

Megendra recited one final incantation, his voice interwoven with Han's. Together they summoned cyclones of wind and lightning that coiled around the Warden, pinning it in a vortex of divine wrath.

Han drew a shuddering breath. His armor reconfigured; the hydro-blade reformed at his wrist, blazing cobalt. Channeling every spark of fury and faith, he leapt—

delivering a scything arc of water and light. The slash tore through the Warden's ribcage, cleaving coral and bone. The grotto erupted in steam and spray. The guardian's opal eyes cracked and dimmed. With a final groan of shattering stone, it collapsed—a broken monument. Driftwood limbs sagged, algae veins dulled, and coral fragments fell like dying petals.

Silence reclaimed the cavern. Han dropped to his knees amid the wreckage, lungs burning, suit vents hissing in exhaustion. Megendra's satisfaction rippled through his thoughts.

"We fucking won," Han rasped.

"Indeed," Megendra replied. "Hold fast. Only one relic remains."

Han retrieved the Pale Circlet. Its filigree glowed softly in the fading phosphorescence. The ancient grotto seemed to sigh—its guardianship ended, its power reclaimed—and somewhere beyond, the world trembled at what was still to come.

15

The cavern of the Coral Warden burned dimly with the last of the algae fire. Han stood at the dias, two relics in hand—the Wraithspike's jagged obsidian and the Pale Circlet's pale gold. Megendra's presence surged again, seizing control of Han's body.

"Now comes the true trial," the mage intoned, his voice echoing against the damp stone. "We must forge these shards, bind them, and quell the two lingering pieces of the spirit of Irithar."

Megendra carved shapes into the air above the relics—sigils of flame, tide, and soul-binding. Ancient threads of magic stirred from the cavern's walls and seawater, the glowing moss intensifying until the chamber swam in violet-blue light.

"The Ritual of Fusion," Megendra began.

"By tide and tempest, flame and frost,

We bind thy fragments, two of lost.

Within these runes, your parts unite—

But not your will, nor dark despot."

He drew a spiral around the Wraithspike, weaving golden runes that clung to the obsidian like molten metal. Tendrils of energy snaked into the blade's jagged core, its edges pulsing in resonance.

Next, he lifted the Pale Circlet and whispered another verse. From it spilled a mournful hum—the echo of Irithar's voice, pleading, tempting. Megendra's eyes flared as he trapped the relic in a cage of sapphire light, the runes burning deep into its surface without melting the gold.

With a final motion, he pressed the circlet to the spike's pommel. Light and water exploded together, fire forged through the tide. The relics fused—gold and obsidian intertwining—until the newly minted Half-Crown of Severed Dominion hovered before them, jagged and radiant.

Then, the temperature plunged. A voice, deep and resonant, filled the chamber:

"I… am not finished."

Han staggered as dark energy coiled through his suit, twisting his vision. The Half-Crown shuddered, and from its heart rose a spectral visage—Irithar the Undying. His phantom face was half-shrouded in decay, eyes burning with eternal hunger. His presence pressed through the chamber like a storm, shoving Megendra's consciousness aside.

He reached out, a phantom hand pushing toward Han's chest. "Give me form, mortal! Your vessel is mine!"

Megendra's spectral hands blazed as he seized control. "No!" he roared. He thrust both arms into the air, drawing from the dias a torrent of ancient flame—soul-fire that burned brighter than any hearth. Chanting the final binding spell, he called out, "Spirit of age, bound in this frame, you shall not walk, nor stake your claim. By sea's embrace and storm's fierce cry, remain within these shards, obey, not deny!"

Bluish-white flames coiled around the Half-Crown, spiraling inward. Irithar's phantom shook violently, howling in fury as Megendra's runes branded its ethereal form. The stormfire constricted, caging the specter within a vortex of light and shadow.

Han felt the crown's power surge through him—its cold bite now seared away, the king's essence trapped within the Half-Crown's heart. The spectral scream rattled the cavern walls, then faded, leaving only echoes trembling through the water-soaked air. Control returned to Han.

Megendra receded to the back of Han's mind. The lights dimmed; silence settled.

"Holy shit… we did it?" Han whispered.

Megendra's voice echoed through him, calm but strained. "For now. Irithar's soul is sealed, not destroyed. Should the final shard be forged, the prison may break. When that time comes, we must destroy him."

Han lifted the Half-Crown. It felt heavier than grief, colder than iron. "Then we must not fail."

"One piece remains," said the mage. "The Blackthorn Crest. And with it, our enemy will make his final move."

They left the cavern, the Half-Crown's runes pulsing like a heartbeat. Outside, the ocean wind carried a warning—the true storm was still to come.

They headed back to Yemen. The last piece was in Ireland—on the Blasket Islands off County Kerry. Inishtooskert, to be exact. Han was already plotting how to get there.

16

Ronin and Tommy boarded their flight back to Honolulu. Han was already thousands of feet above the Indian Ocean, bound for Yemen, leaving the shadows of Socotra behind.

Hours later, Ronin and Tommy stepped into their hotel room. The air was cool, still thick with salt and exhaustion. Amy looked up from the bed, reading their faces instantly. She knew.

They sat and told her everything—the Coral Warden, the battle, the spectral voice of the Fatesworn, and above all, the terrifying power now building in Han and Megendra's crusade. Amy's gaze lingered on Tommy; his presence felt changed—straighter, heavier, touched by something beyond human. She could almost sense the saints watching through him.

After a long silence, Tommy turned to Ronin. "He's in Yemen now. We'll never catch up. And if the Fatesworn Sorcerer couldn't stop him… then he's already got two pieces."

Roland's voice spoke through Ronin's mind, grim and steady. "So, what do we do?"

Tommy leaned forward, eyes fierce. "We go for the third piece. Even if Han fails, someone else will come looking for it. Better we have it—and keep it out of everyone's hands. Maybe Roland can help us destroy it."

Ronin nodded. "We need to find it first."

A slow grin spread across Tommy's face. "I already know. I've seen the map in Thalen's memories. It's in Ireland—the Blasket Islands. Inishtooskert."

Ronin grabbed his phone while Amy flipped open her laptop. Within minutes, she found a convoluted but workable route: Honolulu to Alicante, Spain, then on to Kerry Airport, Ireland.

"Holy shit," she muttered. "These tickets are insane. If I buy both, it drains our savings. I could send just the two of you…"

Tommy shook his head. "Buy them. I'll cover your stay here while we're gone. You'll be safer here than back home when the world starts falling apart. I'll handle the rest when we return."

Ronin and Amy spoke together. "No—we can't ask that of you."

Tommy stood firm. "Yes. If Han gets the second piece and reaches Ireland first—if he gets all three—there might not *be* a world to come back to. I wasn't given these powers for nothing. This is why I was chosen. Nothing else matters. Not money. Not comfort. Just stopping him."

Amy looked at Ronin; he gave the smallest nod.

With a resigned breath, she confirmed the purchase. "You leave at 8:00 AM tomorrow."

Tommy booked the room for another week, making sure Amy had a place to stay while they were halfway across the world.

17

That night, the three of them dined at the Polynesian restaurant under the soft hum of torches and ukulele strings. Fire dancers spun and leapt, their flames painting the night like spirits of the ancient world.

They ate, they laughed, they drank. Yet in each of their minds, one question lingered like a weight: *Will we see each other again?*

They went to bed beneath a star-heavy sky, uncertain of what tomorrow would bring—but certain of one thing: they had chosen their path, and there was no turning back.

They left Honolulu at dawn, bleary-eyed but resolute. The airport lights glowed against the ink-blue sky as Ronin, Tommy, and Roland—whispering through Ronin's mind— checked in for their flight: Honolulu to Los Angeles. From there, they sprinted through a two-hour layover to catch the red-eye to Madrid.

In Madrid's vast airport at sunrise, jet lag and caffeine blurred the hours. Tommy rubbed his temples as they boarded the final flight to Alicante—five more hours across Europe's spine. By the time they landed at Kerry Airport just after midnight, nearly forty-eight hours had passed since takeoff. Each terminal echo and baggage shuffle had felt both endless and urgent.

Outside the small arrivals hall, a mist-coated van waited. Ronin shouldered their packs, sliding behind the wheel. Tommy sat beside him. Fog rolled over the narrow lanes as gulls wheeled under a slate-gray sky, time pulsing between exhaustion and adrenaline.

They reached Dingle Harbor at dawn's brittle edge. Foam-white surf lapped against the rotting jetty where an old skiff rocked in the tide. The boatman—face hidden beneath oilskins—gave a curt nod as they climbed aboard. The engine coughed to life, and they left the mainland lights behind, heading west into the gathering mist.

By the time they sighted Inishtooskert, the sun bled purple across the horizon. The island's beehive huts stood in stark relief, their moss-green roofs glistening. Dry-stone walls snaked through windswept fields, and thorn-bristled hedges rose like ancient sentinels.

They disembarked before a weathered standing stone, its carvings half-eroded by centuries of salt spray. Roland whispered in Ronin's mind, translating the inscription:

"Turn back, child of earth; the thorned crown demands a sacrifice."

Tommy swallowed. "No turning back."

Together, they threaded between drystone huts where crows watched from thatched eaves, their cries sharp as broken vows. At the island's heart, the land dipped into a blackthorn-rimmed hollow. Granite columns funneled the Atlantic gales through a jagged archway slick with seaweed.

Beneath that natural maw lay the cave entrance—jagged teeth of granite framing darkness. Above the bracing, two crossed thorns encircled a crown of ash, and more ancient text warned:

"He who seeks the third shard shall bear its burden, but only after blood binds the wreath."

The shifting air tugged at Ronin's focus. Roland said softly, "Be vigilant."

Ronin nodded. Tommy placed a steady hand on the cave wall. Together, they stepped into the phosphorescent gloom.

Inside, ghost-green moss clung to the dripping stone. Brackish pools mirrored their silhouettes as every footstep echoed like an unspoken prayer.

Deep in the hollow, a circular chamber opened before them. A stone plinth, half-submerged in shallow water, bore the Blackthorn Crest—a twisted wreath of scorched blackthorn wood, its ash-tipped thorns curling like snared fangs.

But they were not alone. Both men's suits activated instantly, armor flowing over them like living metal.

From the shadows emerged two wraith-priests, hulking figures draped in ash-gray robes, faces hidden beneath bark masks. Whalebone knives swung at their sides, and blackthorn branches wove through their sleeves and belts, barbs glinting like pale steel.

A hush fell. Roland murmured, "Steel your hearts. These guardians feed on sacrifice."

Tommy's grip tightened on Saintthorn's hilt. Ronin's knuckles whitened around his sword.

Above them, the archway howled with the Atlantic's roar. Beyond, waves battered the cliffs. And in that charged silence—salt, shadow, and ancient warning—they knew the final trial was about to begin.

18

Han stepped off the tarmac at Socotra's makeshift airstrip, the Pale Circlet and Wraithspike secured in a leather satchel. Megendra's voice pulsed through his thoughts: They are closer than you think.

He jogged across the red dirt toward the charter office, a weathered shack guarded by frayed flags. The Yemeni agent shook his head. "No direct flights to Europe for days."

Han's jaw tightened. He laid the satchel on the counter and closed his eyes. Megendra flowed through his senses, drawing on every eddy of wind and grain of sand. A faint shimmer crossed the agent's weary gaze. Papers fluttered. The man blinked, confused—perhaps forgetting his refusal entirely. Megendra had grown adept at bending more than minds—machines too seemed to obey him.

234

"All right," the agent said, swiping across his screen. "One seat on the midnight to Abu Dhabi, then a hop to London, and from there, a puddle-jumper to Dublin. You'll need ground transport to Kerry."

Han paid without hesitation. As he boarded the twin-prop Caravan, he felt Megendra's satisfaction. We move.

The plane climbed above Socotra's "dragon's teeth" boulders and the vast Dragon's Blood Forest, its crimson canopy fading beneath the clouds. Hours later, the glittering city of Abu Dhabi rose below, gold-lit towers piercing the darkness like prayer candles.

A swift transfer later, Han settled into Business Class on a late flight to London Heathrow. The seat felt cramped, the engines' hum a dull roar in his ears. Yet turbulence, chatter, and airport noise faded away—only Megendra's voice filled his mind.

At Heathrow, he dashed through corridors guided by whispered directions: East wing. Flight 372. Gate 44B. Signage flickered, a staff member frowned, and moments later, Han was boarding a commuter jet bound for Dublin.

He arrived at dawn beneath gray skies. Barely feeling the chill, he sprinted through baggage claim and swallowed a stale croissant on the go. Outside, a gleaming black taxi idled.

"Kerry Airport, please," he panted.

The driver nodded, weaving through narrow roads. Megendra's voice thrummed with unease. They are near the wreath's thorn.

Minutes later, they found a tour guide, and Megendra used his magic to convince the man to fly them to their destination, the chopper lifted on gusting sea breezes, spiraling toward the dark silhouette of Inishtooskert. Below, green fields and blackthorn hedges streaked past. The Atlantic roared louder with every passing mile until the island's beehive huts and drystone walls came into view.

Megendra's tone sharpened. They have arrived. Han knew then that Ronin and Tommy were already there, somewhere among the wind-battered hollows.

The helicopter touched down on a rocky plateau above the ancient archway. Han leapt out, heart pounding. The charred blackthorn carvings loomed below.

"Time to finish this," he murmured, disappearing among the windswept stones, Megendra's shadow trailing behind.

He would not be beaten.

19

Inside the cave, the wraith-priests stood motionless, flanking the final relic—the Blackthorn Crest. Behind it, a lone figure remained still as ash, seated in quiet meditation: the Ashen Monk.

Ronin's suit responded first, liquid armor sliding over his limbs in layers of burnished graphite and cobalt. Tommy's remained dormant. He recognized what stirred beyond the veil of light.

The Ashen Monk stepped forward, passing through the wraith-priests like smoke through still air. His presence drew no threat from Tommy's instincts—only recognition. Ancient knowledge stirred, not learned but remembered.

Seredin Kaelthorn. That was his name. The last guardian of the final shard.

Seredin stood tall and gaunt, limbs long and corded like the roots of a wind-carved tree. His ashen-gray robe hung in worn folds, its hem threadbare from centuries of firelight, frost, and silence. Cinched at the waist with a knot of blackthorn branches, the robe carried relics woven into the belt—faded prayer ribbons, a cracked sigil disc, and the brittle stem of a nightbloom flower, long dead.

The open sleeves revealed ritual scars etched in curling script along lean, wiry arms—sigils of containment, protection, and sacrifice. Both forearms pulsed with a dim charcoal light. At each hip rested whalebone knives, sheathed in bark-lined scabbards polished smooth by age. His boots were simple—elk-hide bound with braided hemp, darkened by ancient loam.

His face was a study in endurance: hollow cheeks, a high brow inked with soot-drawn runes, and long silver hair tied into a solitary tail. But it was the eyes that stilled the soul— riverstone gray, faintly glowing, filled with mournful resolve that burned without flicker.

Ronin's heartbeat slowed. His armor softened, plates retracting slightly as if mirroring his calm.

Seredin's voice was quiet thunder. "Hello, Thomas. I feel my old friend Thalen's light woven into your soul." He lifted a hand, and the wraith priests silently melted back into shadow.

Tommy bowed instinctively, but Seredin gently lifted him upright. "There's no need to kneel. We are equals.

You've come for the final piece of the Crown of Severed Dominion?"

Tommy met his gaze. "We have. Evil has already claimed the other two shards. Their guardians are gone. We came to protect the last one—and if possible, destroy it."

Seredin's laugh was thin, like wind through hollow stone. "I've guarded the Crest for over thousands of years. Many have come. None has succeeded."

Tommy's expression hardened. "This evil is stronger than any who came before. Thalen gave me his powers because he knew."

Seredin waved it off and turned toward the relic— suspended above a worn dias, its gnarled crown of thorns hovering weightless.

"My friend," the monk said calmly, "I possess greater power than either of my brothers. That's why I was left with the final piece."

20

Before Tommy could respond, a crack split the cavern ceiling. Granite sheared loose. Stone plummeted. All three scattered.

Armor snapped around Ronin and Tommy, full-formed and bristling—but too late.

A black naginata—its blade laced with ancient runes— plunged from above like a thunderbolt and speared Seredin through the back, pinning him to the floor just feet from the Crest.

Seredin gasped—not in pain, but in resignation. Then the wind changed.

Han descended through the collapsing hole like a falling star, pulling the naginata back into his suit. Jets of steam and thrumming energy painted the cavern with fury. He landed in a puddle; his armor drew in the water through hidden vents, converting it into a torrent. A blast of liquid force struck Ronin and Tommy, hurling them against opposite walls.

Han advanced—each bootstep echoing with purpose.

Megendra's voice poured from his mouth, cold and triumphant. "No need to struggle, monk. I've spent centuries searching for the runes to contain you."

The naginata flared out of Hans' armor. Piercing the monk again, runes igniting in violet and blue fire. Bands of light coiled around Seredin's body. The monk gasped once more as the energy constricted. His chest heaved—and fell still.

As Han reached for the Crest, the cavern screamed.

The wraith priests lunged from the dark, whalebone knives flashing, their mouths opening in blood-chilling cries—not screams, but spells. The sound cracked through Han's skull, dropping him to his knees as his ears bled. His armor sealed over his head, muting the shrieks to a dull, grinding thud.

Blades hissed from his gauntlets—a hatchet in one hand, a longsword in the other.

With a violent twist, he cleaved two priests in half. But the instant their bodies hit the stone, they doubled—four rose from the corpses, shrieking again.

Megendra seized full control of Han's limbs. His voice tore from Han's throat: "Urere, urere inimicos tenebrarum!" Burn. Burn the enemies of darkness.

Twin jets of blue fire roared from Han's wrists, incinerating the priests where they stood. Ash spiraled up into the vaulted dark.

From the shadows, Ronin and Tommy watched. The shrieks no longer touched them—their suits shielded their minds. They exchanged a single look.

Then, without a word, they charged. Blades drawn. Souls ready.

The guardian was dead. The crown lay exposed. War had come to claim it.

Han stepped over the burning husks toward the fallen relic. As his hand reached out, Tommy's Saintthorn sword whistled through the flames, slicing between Han's fingers and the prize. The blade struck the crown and carried it, embedding it into the far wall. For a moment, it hung dangling against the wet stone.

Han spun—just as both men lunged.

With a wrench, Saintthorn tore free from the wall, the crown falling behind like discarded majesty. The sword flew back to Tommy, hilt-first, whirring past Han's neck by inches. He spun, the gust of its passage whipping steam from his armor.

Tommy caught it mid-stride, the hilt slapping into his palm with bone-deep certainty. A pale blue shimmer pulsed from the blade's core—it had tasted the crown's power, and now it burned for justice.

Ronin stepped beside him, suit sealed tight, stance low and ready. Both fixed their gaze on Han.

Steam hissed from Han's vents like smoldering gills. Megendra's presence shimmered around him, warping the air.

"You're not leaving with it," Tommy growled, his voice like iron on stone.

Han rolled his shoulders, the armor exhaling heat. Twin blades hissed from his gauntlets—one serrated, one a curved axe like a predator's fang. "You think I've come this far just to be stopped by you?"

Ronin's eyes flicked toward the Crest behind Han. "You're not ready for what that crown carries. You never were."

Han's visor narrowed. Megendra's voice oozed through him, ancient and cold. "I am beyond ready. The crown isn't a burden—it's my restoration."

Behind them, the ashes of the wraith priests began to twitch, threads of ghost-light rising from the floor like embers seeking form. The air tightened. The cavern seemed to draw in breath.

Then Ronin moved. The final battle had begun.

21

The Blackthorn Crest spun of its own accord across the stone, clattering once before rolling to a stop. For a heartbeat, all was still—the last embers reflected in Han's visor.

Then he moved.

Han surged forward, jets of steam blasting from his shoulders. His armored boots splashed through puddles as he swept low toward Tommy and Ronin, one blade serrated with honed teeth, the other an obsidian axe.

Ronin intercepted first, gauntlets braced. Sparks flared as Han's strike slammed into his forearm shield, sending him skidding backward and gouging twin furrows across the wet stone.

Tommy was already midair, Saintthorn arcing down in a radiant slash. Han twisted with inhuman speed, jets firing from his back, and met the blow mid-leap. Steel clanged against steel, throwing both apart.

Han landed in a crouch, one hand pressed to the ground. The puddle beneath him rippled, then rose. Water twisted upward in a narrow vortex, coiling around his limbs before exploding outward in a deafening kinetic blast.

The wave hurled Ronin into a granite column, shattering part of his chest plate. Tommy flipped through the surge, cutting its momentum with Saintthorn before landing beside the fallen monk.

Han straightened. "You two can't touch me."

Behind them, the wraith-priests—now ghost-silent—moved not to fight, but to gather. They circled Seredin Kaelthorn's wounded body, kneeling in unison. Their blades rested beside them as their chant began—not in sound, but in spirit. They wove a ward only those attuned to the soul could sense. The monk wasn't dead. Not yet.

Han didn't see. His focus narrowed as Ronin roared and charged again.

Ronin's fists ignited. Vents along his forearms burned crimson as he mirrored Han's stance. His punch met Han's chest plate like a battering ram. Metal screamed. Han skidded backward, catching himself in a reverse cartwheel, jet-boosted legs absorbing the shock.

He grinned beneath his visor. "Finally. You're trying." Then he retaliated.

His palms opened, unleashing twin jets of frigid air. Frost raced across the stone, encasing half the chamber in ice. Ronin's feet slipped. Han's knee slammed into his gut, and a blast from his leg thrusters hurled him across the chamber.

Tommy lunged in, Saintthorn clashing against Han's hatchet again and again, each strike ringing like a struck bell. Sparks flew as the relic blade glowed hotter, feeding on the corruption in Han's soul. The more they clashed, the brighter it burned.

Han hissed. "That sword…it judges me."

Tommy's eyes flared. "It should."

Han batted him away with a burst of strength, then launched a heel-kick that sent Tommy crashing against the wall. The monks' circle behind them glowed brighter.

Ronin reappeared, armor reformed, flanking fast. He slammed his boot into the ground, sending a seismic ripple through the chamber. Han staggered—just long enough for Tommy to flip behind him and swing Saintthorn low.

Han ducked—he was too fast.

Dropping to one knee, he unleashed a pressurized spear of water that blasted Ronin through a pillar of basalt. The suit groaned on impact as Ronin crashed to the ground, breath knocked from his lungs.

Tommy attacked from the side, but Han caught Saintthorn in his gauntlet. The sword locked between shifting finger-spines that writhed like mechanical tendrils. "You don't understand," Han hissed, twisting the blade. "This is evolution. I am evolution."

Tommy only grinned. His hand shot forward, runes igniting across his skin. Blood crystallized into sigils along his arm and chest, burning with divine energy. The strike detonated point-blank, blasting Han off his feet.

Han hit the ground hard. For the first time, he groaned in pain. Then he saw them.

The wraith-priests, fully encircling Seredin now, had formed a cocoon of translucent ash. The monk's body pulsed with faint light. Barbed thorn-roots along his belt dug deeper into the stone.

Megendra stirred in Han's mind. *They're buying time for resurrection. Kill them. Break the circle.*

Han rose to obey—but Ronin was already there. Battered, burning, resolute. His gauntlets split open, forming wide arc-shields that blazed with heat. Tommy flanked him again, Saintthorn glowing white-hot with divine memory.

"We don't need to beat you," Ronin growled behind his visor. "We just need to stall you."

Han turned to strike—just as the chamber erupted in light.

The Ashen Monk was waking.

The cavern thrummed. The Blackthorn Crest lay silent against the wall, glowing faintly—until Seredin Kaelthorn drew a breath that thundered through the stone.

His eyes flared open. The monk's voice, rarely raised, now roared with centuries of contained wrath. "Let. Him. Fall."

A ring of white fire exploded from his chest, a shockwave of pure sanctity. The blast hurled Han backward like a rag of metal, slamming him into the far wall beside the Crest. His fingers fumbled—then closed around it.

The instant his skin met the final piece, the relic ignited. The Wraithspike and Pale Circlet, still fused into the Half-Crown, flew to him like drawn iron. The three shards spiraled together, clicking into place, runes flaring as Megendra's voice filled Han's mind in ancient syllables of binding:

"Formis dominum. Sanguis aeternum. Ad cor meum redeat."

The Crown of Severed Dominion was whole again. And beneath it, a body began to form.

Nine feet tall, gleaming and terrible, armored in storm-forged bone. Silver threads of soul-tendons wove muscle across its frame. When the crown lowered onto its brow, Megendra's spirit poured into it like smoke filling lungs.

But something went wrong. Han froze. His instincts screamed. The new vessel—Megendra's rebirth—was draining him.

Han dropped to one knee, gasping. "It's… feeding on me."

Ronin moved fast. Vaulting over shattered stone, he slammed a gauntlet into Megendra's shoulder and ripped Han free, sealing the breach in his spirit just in time. But it wasn't over.

The pendant—a carved obsidian loop on Megendra's breastplate—still glowed with the Crown's power. It was the anchor for his spells.

Now whole, Megendra raised a clawed hand and began to chant.

"Miserere damnati… Venite domini fracti…"

The air split with crackling energy. The cave shuddered, pillars cracking as dark winds howled through the dust.

Then came the screaming.

Not Han's. Not Megendra's.

The scream of a king long dead.

Irithar.

The final sliver of his soul trapped in the crown had awakened. Megendra's form convulsed, his voice faltering mid-incantation. One eye blazed violet, the other icy blue— two titans warring in the same shell.

Seredin, now fully risen, raised his hand. "Now."

The Monk's barbs uncoiled from his waist, dancing like whips of silver flame. Roland shouted in Ronin's mind, Strike the pendant! It's his tether!

Ronin charged from the left, fists ablaze. Tommy moved from the right, Saintthorn glowing with celestial judgment.

Seredin closed the gap with a burst of spectral speed, his body streaming cinders and prayer.

They hit.

Ronin's gauntlet cracked the armor at the pendant's edge.

Tommy's Saintthorncarved deep, burning with Irithar's guilt.

Seredin hurled his blackthorn wreath like a divine chakram—it shattered the pendant, splitting Megendra's chest open in a geyser of spectral fire.

Megendra screamed as Irithar's presence turned against him. His body seized, lightning writhing through his veins. Both souls howled, clawing at the cracks in reality itself.

Tommy didn't hesitate. He plunged Saintthorn into the Crown atop the vessel's head. Ronin struck at the same instant, channeling all his strength through his fist. Seredin whispered his final prayer: "Forgive the gods, and end their chains."

The Crown of Severed Dominion cracked. Then split. Then exploded.

White light swallowed the chamber. Silence followed.

22

When the light faded, the throne was gone. The vessel— dust. The fragments of the crown dissolved into ash, drifting in slow spirals toward the sea.

Megendra was gone. So was Irithar.

Seredin stood for one long moment. Then, like wind-blown ash, he dissolved—peace finally granted.

Tommy fell to his knees. Ronin dropped beside him, exhausted but alive. Han, coughing against the far wall, looked at the empty space where power once gathered and whispered, "Thank you." Then passed out.

The world didn't tremble when the Crown of Severed Dominion was destroyed. No storms split the skies. No continents cracked open. The gods did not weep.

But those who carried its weight felt it vanish, like a string finally cut.

Ronin stood on the edge of Inishtooskert's windswept cliffs, watching the Atlantic churn below. The sun pierced clouds in golden shafts, and Roland's voice—ever calm—echoed in his mind. You've done what even kings could not.

Then the voice faded—not gone for good, but gone until he was needed again. If he was needed.

Tommy knelt beside the ashes of Saintthorn, the blade now nothing but dust and memory. He could hear Thalen's voice in the back of his mind: Some burdens are sacred. Some souls, too. His hands trembled—not from fear, but from knowing his life had changed again. This time, for good. He had walked the line between miracle and massacre—and chosen salvation.

Han awoke beneath the dawn light, breath shallow, face streaked with soot. The drain was gone. The Crown's shadow had lifted. He sat up slowly, wincing. No armor. No commands. Just himself.

"I'm… still me," he whispered, like a question.

Ronin crouched beside him, offering a hand. "You made a choice."

And Han took it.

23

Back in Honolulu, Amy sat on the edge of the hotel bed, a book in her lap. She looked up as the door opened and saw Ronin first—weary but alive. Then Tommy, quieter now, his smile gentler.

She didn't ask questions. She just hugged them both.

A few moments later, when Han walked through that same door, awkward and unsure, she hesitated only a moment, then nodded.

"You've got work to do," she said. "But you're welcome to start over and earn our trust."

Somewhere beneath the earth—beneath the crusted bones of forgotten kings and hollow gods—the fragments of the Crown slept now. Scattered dust. Useless metal. Not buried.

Just gone.

Because sometimes the most powerful thing isn't what's forged.

It's what we refuse to wear.

EPILOGUE

The world moved on—but not untouched.

Legends of Inishtooskert spread: of thunder heard beneath the sea, of fire dancing on forgotten cliffs. No proof. Just whispers. But some listened. Some watched.

In a sealed chamber far beneath Vienna, a vault long thought inert stirred to life. Dust shifted. A relic—blackened, unmarked, yet pulsing—began to hum again.

In Kyoto, a shrine maiden dreamed of a mountain wrapped in a chain and vine. She woke screaming, clutching a name she did not know. "Kurokaze."

In a small town in Idaho, a child drew a circle of thorns on the wall in chalk. He said it sang to him—in whispers made of fire and ice.

Far above them all, a fragment of Megendra's soul, sealed within a splintered keystone, drifted through astral currents, searching for a host—or perhaps a path back to form.

Ronin thought he was finished. Tommy hoped he was. Han knew better.

None of them has had the dream yet.

But when they did, they'd remember the weight of the crown—and know their work wasn't done.

Just… delayed.

THE END